Blaze

*What could be hotter than a cowboy in June?
How about a cowboy in July, August
and under the mistletoe, too!*

New York Times bestselling author
Vicki Lewis Thompson is back in the
Harlequin Blaze lineup for 2014, and this year she's
offering her readers *even more....*

Sons of Chance

*Chance isn't just the last name of these rugged
Wyoming cowboys—it's their motto, too!*

Saddle up with

#799 RIDING HIGH

(June)

#803 RIDING HARD

(July)

#807 RIDING HOME

(August)

And the sexy conclusion to the
Sons of Chance Christmas series

#823 A LAST CHANCE CHRISTMAS

(December)

Take a chance...on a Chance!

Blaze

Dear Reader,

When I first set foot on the Last Chance Ranch in 2010, I had no idea that one day I'd be welcoming you to the sixteenth book in the series! I know some of you have been with me for the whole ride, and some might be joining me for the first time. Either way, I've worked hard to make sure that each story stands alone. Whether you're a long-time Sons of Chance fan or just beginning to get into the series, you won't get lost, I promise!

After all these books, *Riding Home* seems like an appropriate title. Each time I go back to the Last Chance Ranch, I feel as if I'm coming home. The two-story log ranch house is as familiar as my own house. The Chance family members are friends, and I'm quite attached to the horses, too!

I know from your emails and comments on Facebook that many of you feel the same way. If you read both *Riding High* and *Riding Hard* you know whose story this has to be. Regan O'Connelli and Drake Brewster have found their soul mates, and I think Jeannette Trenton, despite her issues, deserves a shot. I've put her in the path of Zach Powell, a recent hire at the ranch, but he has some demons of his own.

So let's see how they handle the situation, shall we? Of course you'll get to hang out with the rest of the gang at the ranch. Jack Chance can't let a book go by without making his presence known, and Mary Lou always has a fresh pot of coffee available for anyone who shows up in her kitchen. Grab yourself a mug and make yourself at home!

Cozily yours,

Vicki

Riding Home

—

Vicki Lewis Thompson

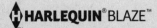

Recycling programs
for this product may
not exist in your area.

ISBN-13: 978-0-373-79811-7

RIDING HOME

Printed in U.S.A.

ABOUT THE AUTHOR

New York Times bestselling author Vicki Lewis Thompson's love affair with cowboys started with the Lone Ranger, continued through Maverick and took a turn south of the border with Zorro. She views cowboys as the Western version of knights in shining armor—rugged men who value honor, honesty and hard work. Fortunately for her, she lives in the Arizona desert, where broad-shouldered, lean-hipped cowboys abound. Blessed with such an abundance of inspiration, she only hopes that she can do them justice. Visit her website, www.vickilewisthompson.com.

Books by Vicki Lewis Thompson

HARLEQUIN BLAZE

+Sons of Chance

To my wonderful readers—
You've taken the Sons of Chance into your hearts,
and your enthusiasm touches me!

Prologue

From the diary of Eleanor Chance
August 15, 1990

WHEN YOUR CHILD MARRIES, you instantly become related to a whole lot more folks. Sometimes that's a lovely thing and sometimes it's not. But in the case of our only son, Jonathan, marrying Sarah Gillespie eight years ago, we lucked out. Judy and Bill are salt-of-the-earth.

When I told Judy that, she called it a supreme compliment. She's lived in Shoshone for more than thirty years, but some locals still think of her as an uppity Easterner. I admit when she first arrived she caused quite a stir, and people around here have long memories.

She blew in from New York City, flush with money from her modeling career and wearing pricey designer outfits. She immediately bought a small ranch and hired one of Jackson Hole's most eligible bachelors, Bill Gillespie, to help run it. We all predicted they'd get married, which they did, and within a year little Sarah was born.

But then Judy made the mistake of announcing she'd only have one child in order to keep her figure. That didn't sit well with the town busybodies. Personally, I didn't give a hoot. She had the right to make that decision for herself.

I liked her from the get-go. She was generous with her money, always willing to support local charity efforts, and she worked right alongside Bill as they turned their place into a cute little guest ranch. She worked hard to make the place cozy and profitable until they chose to sell and move into town.

Judy came over today so she, Sarah and I could have a confab about Jack's twelfth birthday party next month. Judy keeps trying to get that boy to warm up to her, but Jack's a funny one. He's never quite recovered after his mother left when he was a toddler.

Consequently he got it into his head that because Sarah is not his "real" mother, he has no right to claim Judy as his grandmother. He thinks his brothers are the only ones who deserve that privilege. No amount of reasoning works with him. Next to the word *stubborn* in the dictionary is a picture of my grandson Jack.

But Judy keeps trying, and the birthday present she's bought for Jack is a perfect example. She asked a rare book dealer in New York to track down an autographed copy of one of Jack's favorite Louis L'Amour titles. I don't even want to know what she paid for it, and Jack won't realize the effort and expense involved, but I'm sure he'll treasure the book. Maybe someday he'll realize what a gift of love it is.

In any case, I'll be forever grateful that Judy chose Wyoming as her landing spot after she left modeling.

Besides giving birth to the amazing Sarah, she's also been an asset to the community. In my opinion, we could use a few more Easterners blowing into town to shake things up and keep us from getting too set in our ways.

1

ON HIS KNEES inside an empty stall, Zach Powell concentrated on nailing a loose board in place. Except for one horse with medical issues, Zach was alone in the barn. Or so he thought until he stopped hammering and heard the echo of footsteps.

Whoever was wandering around wasn't wearing cowboy boots, either. Boots made a distinctive *clump-clump* sound on the wooden barn floor, whereas this was a sharper *click-click*. After spending years in L.A. courtrooms, Zach was familiar with that noise.

For some reason, this woman was wearing stilettos in the barn. He'd only been working here a few weeks, but he hadn't seen a woman in stilettos anywhere on the ranch, let alone in the barn. He was curious enough to stand up and take a look.

She was five stalls down and totally focused on Ink Spot, a black-and-white Paint who'd been kept in because of a recent sprain. Tall, slender and blond, the woman wore cream-colored dress pants and a lemon-yellow blouse, probably silk. The shoes that peeked out were also yellow and probably designer, judging from the rest of her ensemble—gold bangles on her wrists and gold hoop earrings. No doubt her short, sleek haircut was courtesy of a pricey salon.

She looked completely out of place here, except for the way she stroked the horse's nose. Whoever she was, she knew horses, which made her outfit even more puzzling. She touched the horse with great affection, reaching up to scratch under his forelock as she murmured softly.

Something about the way she communed with Ink Spot told Zach that she wasn't eager for company. He should just finish up his hammering and leave by the back door. On the other hand, she didn't look very happy. Zach knew all about unhappiness.

She'd been so motivated to seek the comfort of horses that she'd risked her expensive outfit by coming out to the barn. That meant she must be really upset, and by speaking to her, he could be intruding on a private moment. Plus, they didn't know each other.

He'd about decided to go back to his hammering when she turned toward him. "You're probably wondering what the hell I'm doin' here dressed like a Sunday school teacher."

No Sunday school teacher he'd ever known had looked like that, but the Southern accent clued him in. This had to be Jeannette Trenton from Virginia. Everybody on the ranch knew her story, even a new hire like Zach.

Last year she'd been Regan O'Connelli's fiancée, but then she'd cheated on him with Regan's best friend, Drake Brewster. Consequently Regan had left Virginia and moved to Wyoming. He was related by blood or marriage to quite a few Chance family members, and they'd all been incensed about Drake and Jeannette's betrayal.

Since then Regan had found a new love, Lily King. Then Drake had shown up to make amends, and in the process he'd become chummy with a local woman, Tracy Gibbons. Drake had also invited Jeannette to Wyoming so the three former friends could bury the hatchet. They seemed to have done that, but members of the Chance family weren't so quick to forgive and forget.

Zach could imagine why Jeannette had come out to be with the horses for a while. Even in his brief time here, he'd figured out that angering a Chance, or someone connected to a Chance, was a huge mistake. He gave both Drake and Jeannette props for braving that disapproval in order to repair their friendship with Regan.

So this was the woman at the heart of the controversy. He had no trouble picturing that, because she was stunning. Apparently she'd known that he'd been staring. Maybe she was used to men looking at her, because if she'd been attractive in profile, she was breathtaking full-on. Those green eyes were showstoppers, not to mention her kissable mouth.

He cleared his throat. "Um, I didn't mean to bother you. I heard you come in, and I thought maybe…" What? His mind went blank. Pretty embarrassing for someone who used to make his living as an entertainment lawyer, someone who'd dealt with A-list actors, directors and producers every day. She didn't have to know that, though. He wasn't that guy anymore.

"I was tryin' to help with the food for Regan and Lily's engagement party, but…" She gestured to her blouse. "As you can see, kitchen duty is not my talent."

He walked closer. Yeah, now he noticed flecks of something that could be meringue or white frosting on the front of her blouse. "It sort of matches your pants."

That brought out a sad little smile. "You know, I told them that very thing, but they were all worried about the blouse, which I surely appreciated, but they don't have time to mess around with a klutz like me. I'd already dropped a bowl of chocolate chips. I thought I could frost that danged cake. I swear, how hard can that be? Turns out it's harder than it looks on TV."

He couldn't help smiling back. "Everything's harder than it looks on TV."

"Isn't that the God's truth? Anyway, I decided to make myself scarce and just naturally gravitated to the barn."

"I completely understand. You obviously know your way around horses."

"My folks raise them." She turned back to the horse. "Who is this, by the way?"

"Ink Spot. He's nursing a sprain, so he didn't get to go out."

"His bad luck, but my good luck. I wasn't thinkin' the horses would be out in the pasture, but of course they would be on a fine day like this. Back home they tend to bring them into the air-conditioning in the heat of the day." She stroked the gelding's neck. "And who would you be?"

Because she wasn't looking at him, he didn't immediately understand she was asking for his name. But he'd already supplied the horse's name, so she had to mean him. "I'm Zach. Zach Powell."

She continued to caress the horse. "I suppose you know who I am." Her version of *I* sounded more like *ah*.

"I didn't until I heard your accent."

She was quiet for a moment. "It's real strange, knowin' that people talk about you behind your back. Of course, people do that all the time. You just don't know it for sure. In this case, I do."

"For what it's worth, I have no stake in this situation. I started working here last month and I'm not related to any of the players." He could add that his law training predisposed him to remain impartial until he'd heard all sides of a story. But for now, he was just a cowhand, and that suited him fine.

"You're new here?" She glanced at him with a spark of interest in her eyes. "Where'd you come from?"

"California."

"Then I'm pleased to meet you, Zach Powell. I have to say you're the first person who hasn't looked at me with thinly disguised suspicion, like I might suddenly sprout horns and a tail. Well, I take that back. Sarah Chance seems willin' to suspend judgment, and her cook, Mary Lou, is friendly. But Regan's sisters…" She sighed.

"Not welcoming?"

"No, and I can't say as I blame them. I don't have a brother, or a sister, either, for that matter. But if I did, I'd probably behave exactly the same way. They're loyal and I admire that. I just…don't know what to do."

"Well…" Zach hesitated. He had some thoughts, but it wasn't his place to make suggestions.

Her gaze sharpened. "What? If you have ideas, speak up. I could use some advice."

"All right. You look great, but you don't exactly blend into the scenery."

"Don't think I don't know it." She glanced down at her outfit. "My mother taught me that wearin' nice clothes is respectful, plus I'd heard that the Jackson Hole area was filled with celebrities so I thought this ranch might be dress-for-dinner sophisticated. I should have asked Drake more questions before I flew out here." She swept a hand down her body. "Everything I packed is like this."

"And Drake didn't say anything once he found that out?"

"We haven't discussed my wardrobe choices. The poor man is so in love with Tracy he wouldn't notice if I ran around naked. Same thing with Regan."

Zach would certainly notice. Thanks to her comment, he was picturing that scenario in vivid detail. He tried to erase the image, but his libido wouldn't cooperate. He hadn't been involved with anyone for months and had thought he didn't miss sex all that much. Judging from the stirring in his groin, he'd missed it more than he'd realized.

To take his mind off the subject, he focused on a potential solution to her problem. "You need to go shopping."

"I think you're right, but I don't know the area. Where should I go?"

"Shoshone has a few shops, but if you want to get what you need, you'd better go to Jackson."

She took a deep breath. "Then I'll just head to Jackson, I guess. Do you recommend any particular stores? No, wait, never mind. I can figure it out. You've been a big help already, and I —"

"I get off at five. Give me time to shower and change, and I'll drive you up there. We can take my truck. Everything stays open late for the tourist trade."

Her shoulders sagged in relief. "That sounds fantastic, but are you sure it's not too much trouble?"

"No trouble at all. I could use a couple of things myself."

"Then I'll pay for gas."

He smiled. "Not necessary."

"No, seriously. And I'll buy dinner. It's the least I can do."

He started to argue with her. He hadn't dated since making this drastic change in his lifestyle. Previously he'd been the high roller who picked up the tab, and having her pay for gas and food felt weird. His wages at the Last Chance were a joke compared with what he used to make in Hollywood, but he'd invested well and didn't ever have to work again if he chose not to.

Unless he planned to explain that, though, he might want to keep his mouth shut and accept her offer. "Okay, thank you. That would be very nice."

"I'm staying at the Bunk and Grub. Do you know it?"

"Yep. Nice bed-and-breakfast down the road."

"It is. Very nice. At first I was in the cabin Drake rented, and he said I was welcome to it now that he's moved in with Tracy. But it's kind of remote, and I'm a city girl. I'm not all that brave when it comes to things like…well, grizzlies."

"Don't blame you. I'm really careful out at my campsite. I keep everything bears might want locked up tight inside the Airstream."

She blinked. "Campsite? You don't live in the bunkhouse?"

"Oh, they offered to put me there. But then I'd have to store the Airstream, and besides, I like living in it. So Jack gave me permission to park down beside the creek that runs through the property."

"Jack Chance?"

He laughed. "The one and only. A legend in his own time."

"So I hear. I haven't officially made his acquaintance. Do you get any electricity down there?"

"I have a little generator. Don't run it much. Mostly I cook over the campfire and I have a solar water setup outside for taking showers."

"Sounds primitive." But instead of looking appalled, which would make sense given her city-girl orientation, she seemed intrigued.

"It works for me." Then it occurred to him that he'd just painted a picture of *him* naked. From the gleam in her eyes, could she be enjoying the image of him standing under that solar shower? Hmm. "So how long will you be sticking around?" He was suddenly more interested in that.

Her jaw tightened. "I'm determined to stay until after the engagement party, no matter how unwelcome I may be." Then she clapped a hand over her mouth. "Did I just say that out loud?"

"You did, but you said it to the right person. I'm not here to judge. I'll bet socializing with this crowd is a bit uncomfortable for you."

"You don't know the half of it. But like I said, I can't blame them at all. I'll tough it out because I want to give Regan and Lily a big hug on their special day. That's important to me."

He wondered if Drake's new romance bothered her. She might have been hooked on the guy and now he'd moved on. "So the party's tomorrow night. Are you leaving Sunday?"

"I didn't want to run off like my danged tail was on fire, so the plan is to fly out Monday."

"I see." Not much time to get to know each other. That was sort of disappointing given that some mutual attraction seemed to be developing.

"And I need to get back to my job."

"Doing what?"

"I'm a lawyer."

"Is that so?" He should get an Academy Award for his casual response. Inside he was laughing his head off. He'd worked so hard to leave that profession behind, and now he was making goo-goo eyes at a member of the clan. The last person in the world he'd ever date would be another lawyer. "What's your specialty?"

"Do you need legal advice?"

"No."

"I ask because usually when I mention that I'm a lawyer people's eyes glaze over. But if they have a legal issue, then they want to know what kind of lawyer I am, either because they might hire me or, in some cases, they're after free advice."

"I know." Whoops. "I mean, I'll bet. But I don't need a lawyer." Not in any sense. "I was just curious. Anyway, you have to survive until Monday."

"I do, but I'm sure more appropriate clothes will help me with that. That's so obvious I can't believe I didn't think of it, although I wouldn't know where to go. The party's being held outside, so jeans would be good."

"And boots." Zach glanced down at her yellow shoes.

"Guess so. These aren't going to work for a barbeque." She lifted one foot to peer at the sole. There wasn't much surface area to the bottom of her stiletto, but the little that existed was dotted with smashed chocolate chips, dirt and bits of straw. "Good Lord." She groaned. "I probably tracked chocolate chips all over Sarah's hardwood floor on my way out."

"Probably."

"Worse yet, the housekeeper is one of Regan's sisters. Cassidy idolizes that brother of hers. She's already wantin' to snatch me bald-headed, and now she'll have to clean up my trail of chocolate. I'll have to go back inside and apologize to her. To all of them." She glanced up at Zach. "You must think I'm a total screwup, but I swear I'm not. At least not normally."

"I believe you."

"Do you?" She met his gaze. "I don't know why. I'm the woman who cheated on my fiancé with his best friend. Then I showed up here in designer clothes more suitable to a country club than a ranch, and obviously I made a mess of things in the kitchen." Her voice caught. "If that's not a description of a screwup, I don't know what is."

She seemed to be on the verge of tears and he considered pulling her into his arms and letting her have a good cry on his shoulder. She probably needed to release some of that tension that had her wound way too tight. But they'd just met, and he also sensed a Southern reserve in her. If he coaxed her into crying it out, she might be horribly embarrassed afterward.

Besides, if she were going back inside to apologize for the chocolate on the floor, she wouldn't want to have red, puffy eyes. He'd only known her a short time, but he could already tell she wouldn't want her vulnerability made public. Unfortunately, her natural reserve might be working against her, too.

So he settled on words of encouragement to shore her up instead of physical contact that would make her lose her cool. "You can't be a total screwup. You flew out here and made peace with your ex. That took diplomacy and guts. Even though you know nothing about cooking, you volunteered to help prepare the food for tomorrow's party while working with women who aren't all in your corner. That takes nerves of steel. I'm just a bystander to this drama, but from my perspective, you're pretty damned incredible."

She stared at him for a long time, her eyes growing suspiciously bright. Then she sniffed and used her thumbs to flick away the moisture gathering on her lower lashes. "Thank you. You can't know how much that means to me."

"Oh, I have some idea. I'm a recovering perfectionist."

Her smile trembled. "I'm just a plain old perfectionist. Maybe on the drive to Jackson you can tell me how to get rid of that tendency because it's a royal pain in the ass."

"I hate to be the bearer of bad news, but you never get rid of it."

"That is bad news."

"But you might be able to cut it down to size."

"Then I want to know how to do that." She held out her hand. "Until tonight. I'm looking forward to it."

"Me, too." He clasped her hand and his adrenaline spiked. Her grip was firm but her skin was petal-soft. He forced himself to let go when all he wanted to do was draw her closer…and closer yet.

Awareness flashed in her green eyes. "See you later, Zach Powell." Turning abruptly, she walked out of the barn without looking back.

He was grateful for that, because he couldn't seem to move. He stood there like a fool and watched until she was out of sight. His visceral reaction to her had him by the throat, or more accurately, by the gonads.

But she didn't need a lover right now. She needed a friend. Even if she had been in the market for a lover, she worked in the profession he'd vowed to avoid. So he'd help her shop, share a nice dinner and that would be that.

2

ALTHOUGH IT WASN'T quite five-thirty, Jeannette came downstairs to wait for Zach in the Bunk and Grub's parlor. Usually someone was in there reading or knitting or texting, but the room was empty. Then she remembered that the other guests were probably gathering on the back porch for the B and B's scheduled happy hour.

She'd attended that event the previous night and had enjoyed herself until she'd received a text from work. Then she'd gone back to her room so she could straighten out an issue at the office, and by the time she'd finished, happy hour had ended. The porch had been deserted.

For a little while, though, she'd been a welcome part of a social occasion. The guests were all from someplace else so no one knew that she was persona non grata in Shoshone. She could go back there now, reconnect with those nice people and have some wine while she waited for Zach. The young woman at the reception desk near the front door could come and get her when he arrived.

But even though that was a pleasant idea, she'd rather stay here and watch for him. She didn't care if she looked eager for the trip to Jackson and the chance to be with him again. She *was* eager. He was her new friend.

In addition to that, he was a beautiful man. At first glance she'd noticed his broad shoulders and lean hips. She'd registered his confident stance. But when he'd moved closer she'd been captivated by the expression in his cloud-gray eyes. His Stetson had shaded his face slightly, but shade couldn't mute the intelligence and compassion in those eyes.

Sure, male appreciation had flickered in his gaze. That was fine. She wouldn't complain about getting that look, which hadn't been sleazy in the least. But it was his sincere compliment that had blown her away. His empathy for her situation was greater than she'd felt from anyone since she'd arrived. Much as she understood everyone's reaction to her, she'd desperately needed someone like Zach to show up.

Bolstered by his understanding and his praise of her courage, she'd managed to walk back into the ranch house with her head high. She'd apologized for her clumsiness and inexperience in the kitchen. She'd apologized specifically to Cassidy for the chocolate smeared on the hardwood floors in both the hall and the living room.

Had it still been there, she would have gotten down on her hands and knees and cleaned it up herself. But the chocolate had been gone—no doubt someone had seen the chaos she'd left in her wake and reported it to Cassidy.

Jeannette didn't want to think about the comments

that must have flown around as the floor was cleaned. Yet when she'd come back into the kitchen, everyone had been perfectly nice to her, including Cassidy. She gave them all credit for that.

But there hadn't been a lot of warmth coming her way, and she'd caught a few exchanged glances that had made her stomach twist. Maybe if she'd gotten to know them prior to the Christmas Eve drama, this situation wouldn't be so awkward. But during her engagement to Regan, she'd only met his parents. There hadn't been time to fly out to Jackson Hole to see his sisters.

Now they were obviously only being nice for Regan's sake, which was admirable. But if they could somehow manage to see past her awful mistake and get to know and like her as a person… No, that was probably asking way too much under the circumstances. She couldn't help longing for it, though.

Before she'd left the kitchen, she'd mentioned the clothes issue and had acknowledged that hers weren't suited to the weekend's activities. She'd told them about the planned shopping trip with Zach, which had caused a few more exchanged glances.

She hoped that eighteen-year-old Cassidy didn't have a crush on Zach. Jeannette didn't want her to be jealous on top of everything else. Cassidy was the only single woman on the ranch, but Zach was too old for her. Jeannette wasn't good with ages, but the crinkles at the corners of his amazing eyes put him at somewhere past thirty.

And that made him the perfect age for her, since she'd just hit the big three-oh this year. Not that she had any business comparing ages as if they had a future together. He seemed very happy to be a ranch hand in Wyoming living in his Airstream. She was very happy as an attorney in Virginia.

But that hadn't kept her from fantasizing about him taking his solar shower in front of God and everybody. Or replaying his kind words to her right before she'd left the barn. In her fantasy they ended the moment with a kiss instead of a civilized handshake.

She was intensely grateful for his encouragement and help, and their relationship would probably only be a platonic one, but he was very handsome. She'd been doing penance for her sins ever since she and Drake had admitted they weren't right for each other. She hadn't gone on a date since, which had been almost eight months.

Maybe she could be forgiven for having inappropriate thoughts about Zach. She wondered if his sensitive behavior had nudged her libido because it telegraphed his potential as a wonderful lover. It was a logical conclusion.

Any man who'd take the time to listen to a woman's troubles and offer to help her solve them would likely also be committed to giving his sexual partner pleasure. He would employ all the skills he possessed in that endeavor. He wouldn't rest until she was utterly and completely satisfied.

Oh, Lord. That concept made her hot. She got up from the sofa and began to pace the small parlor. She'd better rein in her fantasies before he arrived because a man like him would sense her reaction. That would be plain embarrassing.

The receptionist, a slim brunette, left her desk and walked into the parlor. "Happy hour is about to start," she said. "Would you like a glass of wine while you wait? I can bring it to you."

"No, thanks. But that's very sweet." Jeannette estimated the girl was about Cassidy's age and conscientious about her job.

"I like your outfit."

"Thank you." Jeannette had chosen the least dressy combination she'd brought, but even so the ankle pants were beige linen and the black blouse was silk. At least she'd tied the shirttails at the waist in a faux casual way. Her black Ferragamo mules added a good three inches to her height. She'd left off the bangle bracelets and wore the smallest gold hoops she owned. "I'm afraid my clothes don't fit in very well, though."

"They would if you were staying in Jackson. It's more cosmopolitan there. Are you sure you wouldn't like some wine? When Pam's not here, it's my job to make sure the guests are happy."

"She's not?" Jeannette had thought the B and B owner would be on the back porch serving drinks as she had the night before.

"She's spending the night with her husband. Good thing I'm over twenty-one so I can serve liquor." The girl smiled.

"Where's her husband?" Vaguely Jeannette remembered a ring on Pam Mulholland's left hand, but she hadn't seen a husband around.

"Over at the Last Chance. He's the foreman there. Emmett Sterling."

"I did not know about that."

"Some people think it's strange because she didn't take his name and they each kept their own place, but I think it's cool. Well, I'd better head back there before they get restless." With a grin, she whirled around and left the parlor.

No sooner had she disappeared than Zach walked in the front door. For a brief moment he paused to gaze at her, and the air between them seemed to crackle. Damn, he looked good—clean white Western shirt, snug jeans, polished boots and a light gray Stetson pulled low over his eyes.

She took a deep breath and drew in the spicy scent of his cologne. A little spot of dried blood on his chin indicated that he'd nicked himself while shaving. How endearing. Maybe he was a little bit excited about this shopping excursion, too.

He cleared his throat. "You look great."

"For a greenhorn." She picked up her black cloth shoulder bag from the sofa.

"No, just plain great." He walked into the parlor. "I almost hate to take you shopping for jeans when what you have on suits you so well."

"But as we discussed, it's impractical for a ranch barbeque. And although no one's offered to take me out on a horse, I couldn't ride like this, either. Besides…I want to fit in."

"Then let's go." He ushered her through the front door and down the sidewalk to his truck, which turned out to be muscular, black and dusty. "I would apologize for the state of my truck, but it's always like this. Black is the wrong color if you live at the end of a dirt road."

"But aren't dirt roads inevitable if you work on a ranch?"

"As it turns out, yes. I didn't take that into consideration when I bought this baby." He walked with her to the passenger side and opened the door. "At least the inside's clean."

"Nice." The smell of new leather greeted her as she climbed in and buckled up. The seat rivaled the comfort of her Mercedes back home. He'd splurged on this vehicle, and recently, too. She didn't know how much ranch hands made these days, but the job must pay better than she thought or maybe he'd come in to some money. Or he could be up to his ears in debt.

He settled himself behind the wheel, closed his door and started the engine. The truck's deep-throated rumble was decidedly masculine. So was the man sitting next to her, and his cologne tantalized her even more in the enclosed space of the air-conditioned cab.

She tried to remember the last time she'd ridden in a truck. Even though her parents raised horses, the valuable Thoroughbreds were always transported by professionals in semis. Her family drove luxury cars. Even if she had been a passenger in a pickup a time or two, she certainly hadn't been chauffeured by a Stetson-wearing cowboy.

When she'd imagined this trip to Jackson, she hadn't anticipated that Zach's truck would provide a sensually rewarding experience. She'd assumed he'd have an ordinary truck, maybe one with some rattles and worn upholstery. Instead they cruised down the highway effortlessly.

He glanced at her. "How did things go in the house when you went back?"

"Fine. No one's ever been rude to me, but I can tell they're only being nice because they're decent people and they love Regan. So do I, but I doubt they'd believe me if I said so."

He was quiet for a moment. "You're still in love with him?"

"Not *in* love, but I love him as a friend."

"Oh." He didn't sound convinced. "I'm not sure I understand how that works."

"You've never had a close woman friend, someone you loved but weren't in love with?"

"I'd have to think about that. My close relationships with women always seem to have a sexual undertone. Then when we act on that, we have an affair, and after it ends, we're usually not that close anymore."

She wasn't surprised that he ended up in bed with his women friends. One look at his classic profile as he drove this massive truck got her engines running. His hair was a soft brown with enough curl to curve around his ears. She even liked the shape of those ears. Women would naturally want to get their hands on this guy.

"That's the way it often goes," she said. "I'm the last person to brag about my relationship skills. I used to be so proud of my situation with Regan and Drake. I had love and sex with Regan and cherished Drake as a close friend. But a bottle of wine and general dissatisfaction with the status quo ruined everything."

"If you could go back and change that, would you?"

"Good question." She settled into her comfy leather seat. "If you'd asked me that last January, I would have said yes, in a heartbeat. But now I realize the status quo wasn't right, and goin' to bed with Drake was probably my subconscious effort to change it. Regan and I didn't have the bone-deep passion and commitment that would carry us through fifty or sixty years of marriage."

"Did you have it with Drake?"

"God, no!" She laughed at the thought. Talking about this with someone who wouldn't judge was a huge relief. "He had his own reasons for shaking things up, but an undying love for me wasn't one of them."

"He told you that?"

"More or less. I admitted the same thing to him. We were a sorry pair, all right. I should have broken up with Regan instead of getting smashed and having sex with his best friend. But wedding plans have a life of their own. My parents had made a sizable, nonrefundable down payment on the venue. The wedding party had been chosen, and the dresses and tuxes had been ordered."

"You felt trapped."

"Yes." She heard something in his voice. "From the way you said that, I'm guessing you know what that's like."

"Absolutely."

"Did you almost marry the wrong person, too?" That would explain his empathetic response.

"Nope. But I know what it feels like to be going down a road and realize it's the wrong one, but you can't get a handle on how to change it."

"How so?"

He smiled. "Not now. I want to hear your story."

She made a note to ask later. "There's not much more to tell. Drake and I caused a scandal. My folks pretend they've forgiven me, but they haven't. I think Regan has, though. And Drake, Regan and I are *almost* back to normal. I wish Regan's extended family could let it go, but…they may not. I'll have to live with that."

"I predict they'll warm up."

"If I wear different clothes?"

"Won't hurt."

"I found out something right before you picked me up. I thought by staying at the Bunk and Grub, I'd escaped the Chance family's influence."

He looked over at her. "You didn't know that Pam was married to Emmett?"

"Why would I? They don't even live together!"

"Which is apparently how they like it. They married late in life, so they each need their space, except for…well, the obvious."

"Right." And here they were focusing once again on the topic of sex. The cab was roomy, but not so big that she didn't feel his energy across the console. He was a potent guy.

"Pam is also Nick Chance's aunt."

"She is?" Jeannette sighed. "And Regan joined Nick's veterinary practice when he moved out here, so that explains why Pam has been friendly and polite, but never warm. I thought she was simply being professional, but no, she's part of Team Chance. Oh, well."

"What about Drake? You shouldn't be dealing with this alone. Is he getting the cold shoulder, too?"

"Oh, probably to some extent, but he's been here longer, and now he's involved with Tracy, who's very popular, I gather. They may be giving him a pass because Tracy likes him." Her phone chirped, indicating she had a text. "Will you excuse me a minute? I should get that. It might be from work."

"On a Friday night?"

"Oh, yeah. My assistant is dedicated."

"By all means, see what's up."

Jeannette checked her phone, hoping for good news from Erin, her paralegal assistant. Instead Erin confirmed that they had a big hole in their research on the current case. She promised to work through the weekend to plug that hole, which made Jeannette feel guilty. She should be there helping Erin dig up the information they needed to build a solid defense.

But she wasn't there, and so all she could do was text her sincere thanks for Erin's effort. With a sigh, she put her phone back in her purse. Maybe she should change her flight and go back on Sunday, after all.

"Problems?"

"I was afraid we hadn't thoroughly researched a contract dispute, and sure enough, we haven't. The client expects an open-and-shut case, but at this point, there's no guarantee that we'll prevail."

"Tell me about it."

"Why?"

"I might be able to help."

She was touched, but if he made his living as a cowhand, he wouldn't be of much use in this capacity. She didn't want to insult him, though. "I can describe the case, and I appreciate your offer, but I'm not sure that you—"

"I may not be able to help considering that you're in Virginia and every state is different. But it's worth a shot. Contract law has similarities all over the country."

"Yes, but I still don't think—"

"Look, nobody besides Jack knows this, and I'd

rather not broadcast it if you don't mind, but...I was an entertainment lawyer in Hollywood for thirteen years. Contract law is my specialty."

She stared at him. "Well, that sure as hell explains this fancy truck."

3

JEANNETTE OUTLINED THE CASE, which involved a contract for the sale of a registered Thoroughbred foal. Even though he'd never dealt with the intricacies of Thoroughbred racing, he knew contract law. He grasped the essentials fairly quickly and they debated the merits of the case all the way to Jackson.

He'd thought his interest in contract law was dead. Maybe not. The lively discussion with Jeannette was more fun than it should have been if he'd abandoned his profession. In his heart he knew he hadn't totally given up on practicing law.

But his job at the Last Chance satisfied something basic in his nature. He loved working with the horses, repairing things around the ranch, even shoveling shit. The idea of going back to a desk job didn't appeal to him at all.

Before they'd reached the outskirts of Jackson, Jeannette had texted several suggestions to her assistant, Erin, and had received an enthusiastic response. Jeannette laughed and turned to Zach. "She wants to know if I've stumbled upon a hidden law library up in the hinterlands."

He couldn't pretend that wasn't gratifying. "Just tell her you met a burned-out lawyer who still has a few tricks up his sleeve. Maybe none of them will pan out, either. You have a complicated deal there."

Jeannette sent the message and got back an instant reply. "She says I should lasso you and bring you back to Virginia as…" She stopped.

"As what?" Luck was with him and he found a parking space on the square near the Western-wear store. He pulled into it.

"Never mind."

"No fair." He shut off the engine and turned to her. "What did she say?"

Even at this hour, the summer sky was bright, so her blush was easy to see. "As my, um, love slave."

He laughed. "How did she come up with that? I thought we were talking about lawyerly things."

"I might have said that I met a sexy burned-out lawyer."

"Oh, yeah?" More and more, he regretted that she was leaving on Monday.

"You know you are, Zach. I mean, look at this truck. It oozes testosterone."

"Well, that's good. A manly truck was what I was going for. I just didn't figure on the dust." He surveyed the crowded square. "Which will it be, food or shopping?"

"Food. I'll shop better on a full stomach. Besides, now that I know about your background, I have millions of questions about why you're here and not there."

"It's simple."

"I doubt it."

He opened his door. "I promise you it is, but now that you know I have resources, will you let me buy dinner?"

"Absolutely not. If your suggestions work, then you saved my bacon on this case."

"Don't jump to any conclusions. I might have sent you and your assistant down the wrong bunny trail."

"Or not. Assuming you set us on the right track, I owe you way more than a dinner."

"Oh?" He couldn't resist teasing her. After all, she was the one who'd called him sexy. "And what exactly did you have in mind that would repay that enormous debt?"

She met his gaze with a deadpan expression. "My eternal gratitude."

"*Damn.* Guess I'm not quite sexy enough, even driving this big-ass truck."

"Hold on." Her green eyes danced with mischief. "You don't know what my eternal gratitude might inspire me to do."

Lust arrowed through him and centered in his crotch. He took a steadying breath. "Good point. Guess I'd better take your eternal gratitude for now and see how things work out. Let's find some food."

Twenty minutes later they were finally seated in a little Italian restaurant a block off the main square. It was the only place that didn't have a two-hour wait. He should have anticipated that Jackson would be hopping on a Friday night in August, which was still officially tourist season. At least a table for two was easier to snag than if they'd had a larger party.

He ordered a bottle of Chianti and poured them each a full glass. They were on the far side of the square from the Western-wear store and the truck. By the time they ate, walked back around the square and shopped for her clothes, he'd be fine to drive.

Picking up his glass, he raised it in her direction. "Here's to settling your case in your client's favor."

"I'll drink to that." She touched her glass to his and took a long swallow.

He watched her slender throat move, forgetting to drink his wine. All he could think about was pressing his mouth to that ivory skin and driving her wild with his kisses. She'd told her assistant he was sexy. He really wanted to prove that assumption.

"Zach? Are you okay?"

He snapped out of his sexual daze. "Great. Just great."

"You haven't touched your wine."

"I was waiting for you."

"Am I the taste tester? If I keel over, you'll know not to drink it?"

"No, I... Ah, to hell with it. You're beautiful, Jeannette. I've been trying to ignore that, but then you went and told your assistant that I'm sexy. That sort of changed the game for me."

She put down her wine and gazed at him across the small table. "Okay, I'll admit that you fascinate me, especially now that I know you had this whole other life before becoming a cowboy. What happened? Why did you give it up?"

"If I tell you that, I'm liable to lose some of my sexy quotient."

That made her laugh. "I doubt it. Come on. We

have time before our meal arrives, and I really want to know."

He sighed. "Okay, might as well ruin my image sooner than later. I'd been dissatisfied for quite a while, although I wouldn't admit it to myself. Couldn't see myself walking away from all that money."

"That's understandable."

"Nice try. But it's not understandable when you figure I'd socked away enough to live comfortably for the rest of my life."

Her eyes widened.

"*Please* don't be impressed."

"I'll be impressed if I want to."

"No, seriously, don't be. You can make crazy money in Hollywood. But it's a hectic life and your values can easily get skewed."

"Sure, for the stars, but—"

"For anyone working in the business. I wasn't morally bankrupt, at least not completely, but I was the contract lawyer for someone who was. He was a horse's ass who never showed up at the set on time or else he'd be drunk, stoned or both. The studio finally fired him, but I got him the money, anyway. Millions. He sent me a case of Dom Pérignon and a pricey call girl."

"Wow."

"For the record, I kept the champagne but sent the call girl home."

"You must be a damned good lawyer."

"Used to be. Past tense."

"That seems like a shame." She picked up her wine and gazed at him over the rim of the glass. "All that education and experience, going to waste."

"You're not the first person to mention that."

"I mean, sure, I can understand wanting to leave L.A. if you were burned out from that lifestyle, but you could set up shop somewhere else, especially if you have savings."

"Just can't get excited about doing that."

"So you became a ranch hand, instead. Why?"

He sipped his wine as he thought how to answer without sounding starry-eyed. "I've been around Hollywood enough to know that the cowboy fantasy is a myth created by books and movies. But it's a good myth, and it has some basis in fact."

"Maybe it does." Her green gaze became thoughtful. "Regan once said the guys he met at the Last Chance lived up to the image of what a cowboy should be—brave, honest, protective. I'm not surprised he's happy to be part of that mystique. He's all of those things." Regret shone in her eyes. "He didn't deserve—"

"Hey." He leaned toward her. "He didn't deserve ending up with the wrong person, either. Because of your actions, he didn't. I propose a moratorium on guilt, at least for tonight."

"Okay, but that goes for you, too. I hope you're not still feeling guilty about the money you won for that actor."

He thought about that. "I am, but you're right. I need to lose the guilt. It's over. Can't do anything about it now."

"Right."

"Anyway, the reason I wanted to become a ranch hand is that cowboys are considered heroic, and I wanted to feel like that." He shrugged. "Stupid, huh?"

She shook her head. "No," she said softly. "Sweet."

"Ugh. No man wants to be called sweet. The sweet guy is the best friend of the dude who gets the girl. Everybody who watches movies knows that."

"That depends. Sometimes the sweet guy has a very good chance of gettin' the girl."

"He does?" Zach tried to read her expression to see if she was teasing him or not. The light had faded outside and the restaurant was lit by little candles that cast shadows everywhere.

"I'd say so." She drained her wineglass and put it down carefully on the table. "I've been under a lot of stress lately, but bein' with you is the most fun I've had in a long, long time."

"Then I'm glad I suggested this."

"Life's not so fun when you don't like yourself very much. Sometimes I don't know if people really are disapproving of me or if I'm projecting my own feelings onto them. But I've never sensed disapproval from you."

"Like I said, it's not my place to judge."

"Yes, but not judging is a neutral position. You go beyond that to offer support to the person with difficulties—namely, me."

"Maybe because I know what it's like to live with regrets, especially for those of us who expect a lot of ourselves."

She took a deep breath. "It *sucks*."

"Yeah."

She regarded him silently for a moment. "I've only known you for a little while, but I think we have a lot in common. The lawyer thing took me by surprise, but now it makes even more sense that we click."

"Yeah." He grimaced. "Rotten timing for two people to click."

"Tell me about it."

He looked into her eyes, and his breath caught as he recognized longing…and heat. Oh, yeah, lust simmered just beneath the surface, and he responded, despite himself. A wise man would look away, pick up his wineglass, change the topic.

But he'd been a fool for less important things. His heart pumped faster. "Or maybe it's the perfect time." He reached across the table and took her hand. She sucked in a breath. Clasping her hand between both of his, he massaged her soft skin. "If you could have anything you wanted right now, what would it be?"

"Oh, Zach. Don't ask me that."

"I am asking. Tell me."

She took a shaky breath. "I would love…a break from all of this drama…with someone who's not a part of it."

"Like me." His body warmed, tightened.

"Yes, but—"

"I can do that. Let me give you that tonight."

Her eyes glowed with excitement for a brief second, and then she closed them and shook her head. "I don't want to make another mistake."

"How can it be a mistake? You're free. I'm free. No one ever has to know."

She opened her eyes and met his gaze.

"This is between you and me." He tightened his grip on her hand. "It's our business. Nobody else's. I'm a lawyer. I understand confidentiality."

Her smile trembled. "I'm sure you do." She sounded breathless.

"Just say yes and leave the rest to me."

"I'm so tempted…."

"Let yourself be tempted. Let yourself go."

She stared at him for a long time as a blush crept over her cheeks. "Okay."

"Okay." Now he was starting to shake. "Are you still hungry?"

"No." She swallowed. "To be honest, I haven't wanted a man this much in…I don't know how long."

"Then let's get—" Belatedly he remembered the original reason for this trip. "Wait. You still need those clothes."

"I'll be a power shopper."

"Sounds good. Let's head out." He reluctantly let go of her hand and signaled for the waitress.

She hurried over. "Your order should be ready any minute. We're a little backed up in the kitchen."

"Actually, we're going to have to leave."

"I can have it packaged to go, then."

"Fine." He hadn't figured out the details of the evening yet, so maybe that would work.

"Just give me a few more minutes." The waitress left.

Jeannette scooted back her chair. "I have an idea. You wait for our dinner and the check and I'll head on over to the Western-wear store you pointed out. No need to bore you with the shopping."

He couldn't imagine being bored as long as she was around. But she was right about conserving time. "All right."

She reached for her purse. "Dinner's still on me, so I'll just—"

"You will *not* leave money for the bill."

She paused in the middle of digging for her wallet and gave him a tiny smile. "Okay, I won't. And FYI, your take-charge attitude is very sexy."

Lust slammed into him so hard it was a wonder he didn't gasp out loud. Getting through the shopping would be tough, but if they didn't handle that now, they never would.

"Meet you at the store."

"See you then." The minute she walked away from the table he pulled out his phone. He'd made the transition from mover and shaker to good ol' boy, but that didn't mean he'd forgotten how a mover and shaker handled situations like this. If Jeannette liked his take-charge attitude, she was gonna love the idea he'd just come up with.

Because of the number of tourists in town, he had to make several calls, but within ten minutes he'd booked a luxury suite at one of Jackson's finest hotels. He hadn't experienced that brand of pampering since leaving L.A. and he hadn't missed it at all. But then, he hadn't entertained a woman since then, either.

When the waitress arrived with their takeout order, he paid for the meal they wouldn't be eating and returned the bag with his apologies. He gave her an extra large tip and hoped she'd find a home for that food. He wasn't going to haul doggie bags into a five-star hotel with excellent room service.

By the time he left the restaurant and started toward the clothing store, he was feeling in control of the proceedings. A gorgeous woman had agreed to spend the night with him and that was reason to celebrate.

Oh, hell. He stepped to the edge of the sidewalk

so he wouldn't block traffic and pulled out his phone again, doing a quick web search. Fortunately there was a drugstore a couple of blocks away. He made the journey in record time and tossed the small bag into the truck before heading back toward the Western-wear store.

Jeannette was checking out when he walked in. She glanced up. "Hi. I was beginning to think I'd lost you."

"Not a chance."

She handed her credit card to the clerk. "What took so long?"

"I'll tell you on the way." He joined her at the checkout counter. "Find everything?" Looked like it, judging from two large bags sitting there.

"I did."

"Boots?"

"Yep."

"Hat?"

"I love my hat. It's white straw. I think you'll like it." She signed the credit-card slip and tucked the receipt in the bag. "Ready?"

"More than you know." He was on fire for her. "I'll take those bags."

"Thank you." She hesitated. "So now…"

"You said you liked my take-charge attitude."

"I do."

"So I've taken charge."

4

JEANNETTE FELT ENERGY pouring from Zach as he helped her into the truck. Then he took her bags and stowed them in the covered truck bed. Finally he climbed into the driver's seat and closed the door.

But instead of buckling himself in, he laid his hat on the dashboard, turned toward her and unfastened her seat belt.

She gasped at the unexpected move. "Aren't we leavin'?" She thought he was as eager to get on with the evening as she was.

"In a minute." He cupped her cheek in one large hand. "I need to do something first."

She looked into his eyes, warm with emotion. He planned to kiss her, and how she longed for that. But she was afraid once they started kissing, they would never stop. "Maybe we shouldn't…" She lost track of what she'd meant to say as he stroked his thumb gently over her cheekbone. His touch was heaven.

"Yes, we should. We're about to become lovers, but we haven't even kissed."

"Except we're in the middle of the town square."

"I know." He leaned closer. "We'll be fine."

"What if we get carried away?"

The corners of his beautiful mouth tilted. "*I* won't."

"You might. I'm a pretty awesome kisser."

"Prove it."

She never could resist a challenge. She craved the feel of those sculpted lips on hers even if they were taking a risk making out in a public place. "All right." She grasped his head in both hands. His hair was exactly as soft and silky as she'd imagined. "Come here, you."

He was extremely obliging. In the very next second he covered her mouth with his. Too late, she discovered that she might be the one who would get carried away. She was in the presence of a master.

From that first velvet contact, he was fully in charge. Her world narrowed to the pressure of his lips, the glide of his tongue, the warmth of his breath. His kiss tasted like all the decadent pleasures she'd dreamed of having with a man and had never quite had.

And she wanted those promised pleasures. Her body ached for them. She tried to get closer and came up against the console. She moaned in frustration and writhed against the supple leather of the seat. She needed…more.

Slowly, with obvious reluctance, he eased away. But then he returned to nibble and lick as if he couldn't make himself abandon her mouth. She didn't want him to, either.

"We have to go," he murmured between quick kisses.

"Not yet." She pulled him back for another deep,

passionate round that left her panties wet and her heart racing.

When he finally broke away, he was breathing hard. "We really have to go."

"I know, but…" She tried to tug him down again. "One more for the road."

He resisted her efforts and loosened her grip. "Buckle up. We're getting out of here."

With a sigh, she leaned back and buckled herself in as instructed.

"You were right, by the way. You're a pretty awesome kisser." He started the truck, checked his mirrors and backed out of the parking space.

"Ditto. Um, I suspect you have everything figured out, but where are we going?"

"I booked us a room." He said it casually as he navigated through traffic with practiced ease.

She shivered in excitement. "I should help you pay for—"

"Don't even think about it."

"Okay." She wanted to ask where this room was, but figured he wanted to surprise her. Considering his previous job and the luxury of his truck, she didn't think they'd end up at the cheap sleep.

Watching him drive the huge truck with quiet confidence was very arousing, as was this latest gesture of his. She'd made a veiled request for a sexy timeout, and he'd handled the details. In doing that, he'd increased his hotness by at least a thousand percent.

"That's what took me so long while you were shopping. Well, that and my own shopping."

"Right." She had trouble making casual conversation when her body was humming with anticipation, but she gave it her best effort. "You said you had to pick up a few things, but I thought you meant clothes from the Western-wear store."

"Not clothes."

"Then what...? *Oh*." The electricity arcing between them was almost visible. "Is there anything you haven't thought of?"

"You'll have to do without makeup in the morning."

In the morning. They'd make love all night. She had trouble sitting still. "That's what you think." She always kept an emergency makeup kit in her shoulder bag.

Judging from the looks of the entrance where he turned in, they were staying in a luxury resort. "You sure know how to dazzle a girl." If she sounded a little breathless, she figured she had cause.

"I'm under a time constraint. If I don't dazzle you now, I might never get a chance."

"Trust me, you're way up there on the dazzle meter."

"Good to know." He pulled under the portico for valet parking.

While a doorman helped her out of the truck, Zach retrieved her shopping bags from the back. She'd never checked into a hotel with only two shopping bags, but Zach treated the experience calmly, as if he did it all the time. She suspected he was giving her a glimpse of the L.A. lawyer he used to be.

He might be used to swanky one-nighters, but she wasn't. She'd certainly stayed in plenty of hotels like this, though. Her parents wouldn't accept anything less when they traveled.

But tonight she was checking in with a guy wearing jeans, boots and a Stetson. He was an irresistible combination of sophistication and down-home earthiness. His assumption that this was all perfectly normal made her wonder about his past.

Maybe she'd ask him. Then again, maybe she wouldn't. It didn't matter. This was one night, not the start of something significant.

Once she and Zach stepped into the glittering elevator, he transferred both shopping bags to one hand so he could pull her close for a quick kiss. "Is this working for you?"

"If you mean am I impressed out of my mind, yes, it's workin' for me."

"Good." He gazed down at her as the elevator kept climbing. "In case I forget to say it, thank you for deciding you'd like to spend the night with me."

"You're welcome, but I have the feeling I'll be the one feeling thankful when this is all over." The elevator pinged to a stop and she noticed they were on the top floor. "You rented the *penthouse?*"

"It was all they had."

"Zach!" She stepped out of the elevator and her wedge heels sank into thick carpet. Ahead of her, double doors stood open and she walked into a living area furnished in sleek leather and polished wood. The lamps may have been on a dimmer switch since the light was muted and atmospheric. Floor-to-ceiling windows looked out on the lights of Jackson and shadowy mountains in the distance. "This must have cost a fortune."

"I don't care."

She glanced at a wet bar on the far side of the room. Champagne sat in an ice bucket on the granite counter, along with two crystal flutes and an elegantly arranged cheese-and-fruit platter. She turned back to him. "Seems a shame it's only for one night," she said softly.

He dropped the bags at his feet and sent his hat twirling toward a lamp. It landed precisely on the finial. He walked toward her, his gaze intent. "Then we'd better make the most of it."

If she'd been prone to swooning, she might have done it then. No man had ever treated her like this, as if she were everything he ever wanted, as if every moment they were together was more precious than his next breath. Such a fantasy couldn't last, of course, but it might hold up for a few hours. Then she'd have her unspoiled memory to relive as she reentered the real world.

She spread her arms. "I'm yours for the night. What do you want to do first?"

He laughed. "If you have to ask, then you haven't been paying attention."

"I don't have to ask." If he could act with flair, so could she. "Stop right there."

He paused. "I had in mind something involving bodily contact."

"Me, too, but let's build up to it."

"I've been doing that ever since you agreed with me in the restaurant that this is the perfect time. Before that, if I'm being honest. When you came into the barn this morning you mentioned that Regan and Drake wouldn't notice if you ran around naked."

"I guess I said something like that."

"You said exactly that, and immediately I pictured you that way."

The luxurious setting, the stress of the past eight months and the gorgeous man standing before her made for an electric combination. She was ready to kick over the traces. "Then let me make that picture a reality, cowboy."

He started forward. "I can help."

"No." She held up her hand to stop him. "You'll get the full effect if you stay where you are and watch."

He swallowed and clenched his fists, as if he had to do that to control himself. "Okay."

Knowing how much he wanted to touch her gave her courage to put on a show for him. She'd never felt inclined to do that for a man. But Zach, with his classy ideas and his passionate kisses, inspired her to new heights of sensuality.

Standing in the living room of this expensive suite made the adventure even more exotic. She wasn't in a bedroom doing this, but in an elegant living area with floor-to-ceiling windows. They were too high up for anyone to see in, but stripping down here felt much more risqué than if she were in a smaller room with the drapes closed.

She started by untying her shirttails. She didn't rush it, either. From there she unfastened the mother-of-pearl buttons down the front. Although she'd had the blouse for a long time, she'd never appreciated the sensuality of sliding those buttons free, one by one.

Zach's chest rose and fell more rapidly with each button. When at last she slipped the blouse from her shoulders and let it drift to the carpet, he moaned. That sound caused her nipples to tighten.

Instinct made her touch herself through her black lace bra. She stroked in a circular motion and watched his eyes darken to the color of storm clouds as he focused on her lazy caress. Then she cupped her breasts and in one dramatic gesture, opened the front clasp and shrugged out of the garment. It, too, fell to the floor at her feet.

The sound of his ragged breathing filled the silence, but he stayed where he was, muscles rigid and hands fisted at his sides. The material of his fly strained over his growing erection, and his gaze was so very hot.

She'd never felt so powerful in her life. She nudged off her shoes and unbuttoned her pants. Her hands trembled, not from nervousness, but from the adrenaline rush of knowing she was driving Zach crazy.

She was no expert at this striptease routine, but it didn't matter. For one night she could do anything and be anything she wanted. Just as he'd said in the restaurant, it was their business. Nobody else's. That kind of freedom was a whole new experience for her, but she was catching on fast.

Peeling down her pants, she eventually kicked them aside and stood before him wearing only a tiny scrap of black lace. His attention was riveted on that lacy triangle. She knew he wanted it off, but she had other ideas.

She'd never done this, either. But she'd never have a better reason than now, in this luxury suite with this fascinating man who was almost a stranger. She slipped her hand inside her panties.

Zach sucked in a breath.

"I won't make myself come." She hardly recognized her own voice. It was low and sultry, the voice of a temptress. "I'll let you do that."

"Please." He sounded desperate.

She continued to fondle herself. "Tell me what you want."

"You know." The words came out tight and hard.

"Tell me."

"I want to put my mouth where your hand is. I want to make you come. God, Jeannette…"

"That could be nice."

His jaw tightened. "I promise it will be."

She withdrew her hand and deliberately licked her fingers. "Will I get to return the favor?"

He groaned. "*Yes*, so now can I—"

"Yes, you may." And she slipped off her drenched panties and kicked them away.

He wasted no time. In two strides he was there, kneeling at her feet, splaying his hands over her bottom as he nuzzled his way to the epicenter of all her pleasure. She'd known from the way he kissed that he'd be amazing at this, too.

But as he loved her, as her legs threatened to give way and she clutched his shoulders for support, the word *amazing* didn't begin to describe the sensations rocketing through her. He took charge once more, and she was helpless to control her response.

Her gasps became whimpers, and her whimpers grew in volume. When he paused, she wailed in frustration. His soft laughter told her he was teasing her, testing her. She failed the test because she shamelessly begged for more.

He gave more, of course. He was only giving as good as he'd gotten, gently torturing her as she'd tortured him. But in the end, he finished what he'd

started and she came in a glorious cascade of pleasure. So good. So very good.

He guided her trembling body down to the thick
carpet. Dazed by the force of her climax, sounds traveled to her as if she were underwater. She vaguely
registered the clink of his belt buckle, the rasp of his
zipper and the crinkle of foil.

His mouth found hers, and he tasted of sex. He
kissed her for a long time before raising his head.
"You don't have to do anything," he murmured. "Just
lie there. But I need…" He eased between her thighs
and the blunt tip of his cock sought the hot, quivering
spot he'd loved so thoroughly with his mouth. "This."
He slid deep with a heartfelt sigh. "Oh, yeah. This."

Little shock waves of delight zinged through her
as he locked himself in tight. Then he began to stroke
in and out and she didn't even have to think about it.
She wrapped her arms around him and lifted to meet
each thrust.

"Ah, Jeannette," he murmured in her ear as he increased his speed, "you're with me."

"Yes." She matched his pace and felt another orgasm building.

"I can't… I don't think I can wait."

"Don't wait." Sliding her hands down, she gripped
his firm buns, pressing her fingertips into his solid
muscles as he pumped steadily. His rhythmic movements excited her even more. "I'm right behind you."

He began to pant. "Damn, you feel incredible.
If you didn't feel so great I could hold off, but I…I
can't… I have to… I'm…" With a soft curse, he moved
faster yet.

His excitement fueled hers. She kept up with him as

he pounded into her, and when at last he cried out and drove home, she erupted at the moment his spasms hit. She held on tight as his body shook in time with hers. His groan of satisfaction brought her overwhelming joy, the kind of incandescent happiness that made her toes curl.

She had no idea how long they lay on the floor, but she had no inclination to move. She'd slept on beds that weren't as cushioned as this carpet.

Eventually Zach propped himself on his forearms and gazed down at her with a smile. "You know, this is funny."

She reached up and traced that smile with her fingertip. "Why?"

"I booked this room so our first time together could be on a high-end mattress on a king-size bed. And look at where we are."

"Are you complaining?"

"Never." He leaned down and kissed her on the nose. "But since we've had the floor experience, I vote we conduct the next round in bed."

"And when do you anticipate the next round will start?"

Levering himself higher, he swept a glance down her naked body. He rested on one arm and cupped her breast. Her nipple responded to the lazy brush of his thumb. "Might not be long."

Deep within her body, she felt the twitch of his cock.

He continued to play with her breasts, and the twitch came again. "Might not be long at all." He looked into her eyes. "If we don't have much time together, I don't want to waste any of it."

"I don't, either." But now she saw the fatal flaw in his otherwise excellent plan. They'd created a ticking clock, not unlike lovers had in wartime, where every moment could be their last. That might make this time with Zach seem more significant than it was. She'd have to guard against that kind of delusional thinking.

5

ZACH TALKED JEANNETTE into staying put while he disposed of the condom in the half bath off the living room. He buttoned and zipped his jeans but decided to take off his belt and his boots. They would only be in the way for his next maneuver. Glancing around, he located the bedroom door.

After his somewhat ungentlemanly behavior, taking her on the living room floor, he hoped to redeem himself by masterfully carrying her into the bedroom. He was pretty sure he could manage it. He'd always kept in shape, and he'd just spent a month doing manual labor. But when he crouched down and started to scoop her up, she protested.

"Never mind. I can walk."

"But then I don't get to show off my cowboy muscles. After shoveling out stalls for a month, I'm practically Mr. Universe. Come on. I've always wanted to try it. Humor me."

She smiled and wrapped her arms around his neck. "Okay, if it'll make you happy."

"It will. I might even beat my chest afterward."

"Oh, good. That would be fun to watch. I'd think it would hurt, though."

"Don't know. Never tried it. I'm new at this he-man stuff." From gym workouts and slinging hay bales, he'd learned to lift with his legs. He stood without too much wobbling, and there he was, holding a naked Jeannette in his arms. What a great feeling. "I like this."

She nestled close and gazed up at him. "There's a certain Tarzan-and-Jane quality to it."

"Yeah." When he'd made his living with his brain, he'd kept his gym membership so his suits fit better. But he liked having the strength to pick up his lady love and carry her off like a conquering hero. Very retro and not particularly enlightened, but he couldn't deny the satisfaction of being able to do it.

"Are you takin' me somewhere? Or did you just want to stand here a while?"

"Oh, I'm definitely taking you somewhere." He headed for it with what he considered a purposeful stride.

He laid Jeannette on the chocolate-brown comforter and stood back to admire the view.

"Isn't this the part where you beat your chest?"

"I'm over the Tarzan thing. Now I feel like Rhett Butler carrying Scarlett up the staircase."

"Just so you don't expect me to make a dress out of the curtains. I can't sew. In fact, I'm a washout at domestic chores. Cooking, cleaning, sewing—I'm clueless."

"I don't expect you to make a dress out of the curtains. In fact, that would probably get us permanently banned from this hotel chain." He sat on the edge of the bed and allowed his gaze to travel deliberately over her creamy skin. Under his scrutiny, she flushed a tempting pink. He loved that he could make that happen.

"What *do* you expect?" She asked the question with a twinkle in her eye.

"I have no expectations." He flattened his palms on either side of her head as he leaned closer. "Only give what you feel like giving."

She cupped the back of his head. "I feel like givin' you a big ol' kiss. How's that?"

"I'd like that."

She guided him down, and he delved into the richness of her mouth. In seconds his cock was hard. And he'd left the box of condoms in the other room. He hadn't planned that very well.

He lifted his mouth with great reluctance. "I want you again, but I left the—"

"Never mind."

"But—"

"You promised I could return the favor." And she reached down and unfastened the metal button of his jeans.

A man would be a fool to argue with a proposition like that, and he was no fool.

She pushed gently at his chest. "Just lie back and let me make you feel real good."

The words were seductive enough, but when delivered with a Southern accent…he was a stick of dynamite ready to explode and she'd barely touched him. Stretching out on the comforter, he prayed that he wouldn't embarrass himself by coming right away.

He closed his eyes and gritted his teeth as she fumbled with his zipper and his briefs, but he understood the problem. It was generally better to take the clothes off *before* expansion began. Now that he was fully erect, dealing with the zipper was tricky.

But she finally accomplished her mission. And oh, dear God, the sensation when she wrapped her warm fingers around his shaft made his eyes roll back in his head. He groaned and tightened his jaw against a climax that was perilously close.

"You're gorgeous, you know." She squeezed his cock gently with one hand and reached to cup his aching balls with the other.

"Mmm." It was the best response he could make under the circumstances. Not that he was complaining about the circumstances. These were most excellent circumstances.

He was just worried that… Sweet Jesus, she was using her mouth. She knew how to do that, too. She understood the male anatomy very well, apparently. He clutched two handfuls of the comforter and gasped for breath.

"Good?"

"Yeah." He dragged in more air, but it wasn't enough to carry him through the next deep groan as she took him all the way to the back of her throat. When she flattened her tongue against the ridge on the underside of his cock and began to bob her head in a steady rhythm, he knew the end was near.

Sure enough, she increased the pressure. More, a little more…ahhhh. He surrendered. Loudly. His moans grew even louder as she continued to suck on his pulsing cock. He'd never come so hard or so long, and she'd swallowed every drop.

As he lay there panting, she carefully tucked his family jewels back in his briefs before buttoning and zipping his jeans. Then she crawled up to place a flavorful kiss on his mouth before drawing back again.

He opened his eyes to find her chin propped on her fist as she watched him. He searched for what to say, but nothing in his vocabulary was good enough. "I'm speechless," he murmured. "That was…" He shook his head. "I can't think of a word."

"Super?"

"Better."

"Super-duper?"

"Better."

She smiled. "There's nothing better than super-duper. That's the highest level of excellence there is. Everybody knows that."

He tucked his hand behind his head so he could see her better. "Then let's say super-duper to the millionth power."

"Now you're just being silly."

"Hell, no. There was nothing silly about what you just did. My heart's still going a mile a minute."

"That's what I wanted. To give you a joyride."

"Oh, you did. But I wonder if I'll ever move again."

"You're just low on energy because we haven't eaten."

"That's true." His conscience pricked him. "Are you hungry now?"

She nodded.

"I gave away our Italian meal."

"I wondered where it was."

"I couldn't see hauling cold pasta up to the penthouse. There's a cheese tray sitting on the wet bar, but I think we need more than that. Let's order room service."

"I'll go find the menu. You stay here and recover from your super-duper blow job." She started to move away.

He caught her wrist and tugged her back. "No, I'll go."

"Why should you? I'm perfectly capable."

"I know you are. But I carried you in here in true manly fashion. If you just walk back into the living room, you'll cancel my heroic effort."

"So I'm supposed to lie here like Cleopatra on her barge while you fetch everything?"

"Yes." Taking a deep breath, he pushed himself to a sitting position. "That's exactly what you should do. While I'm at it I'll bring in the champagne bucket, the flutes and the cheese platter."

"We're goin' to eat and drink in bed?"

"I thought we would. Is that a problem?"

"We might make a mess."

"We might." He suspected he'd just uncovered one of her perfectionist tendencies, one that wouldn't risk eating in bed and getting food on the sheets. "Would that bother you?"

She hesitated, but then a defiant light flared in her green eyes. "No. No, it won't."

"Are you sure? Because we don't have to. If you really want to eat at the table in the living room, I won't make you stay here. I was sort of teasing, anyway."

"I *want* to eat in bed. That was the old me popping up, the one who always has to eat at an actual table, the one who worries about food stains on sheets, whether they're mine or they belong to a hotel. The new me, or at least the *tonight* version of me, doesn't care about those things. Bring it on."

"Okay." He wished that they had more than one night together. He'd like to watch this transformation continue. "Then I'll be back in a flash with everything we need."

"In one trip?"

"Sure."

"This I've got to see."

"Prepare to be amazed." He slid off the bed and stood. He was still a little wrecked, but she was probably right about needing food. He wanted to keep up his strength. The night was young.

As he walked out of the bedroom, he marveled that he would be spending the entire night alone in this suite with Jeannette. He had trouble believing they'd just met, because he felt as if he'd known her a long time. Some said if you found the right person, you'd know it instantly.

He wasn't sure he agreed with that, but if there were any truth to the idea, then he'd experienced that immediate recognition with Jeannette. Even her body was familiar to him. He'd teetered on the brink of insanity during her striptease, but every time she'd revealed another lovely part, he'd thought, *Oh, yeah, there you are.*

Weird. But they only had this one night, and she was going home Monday. He needed to remember that. There was no reason to believe she'd changed her mind. This wasn't a movie where she'd get all sappy and run back to him right before she boarded her plane.

He found the room-service menu on a large desk in

a far corner of the living room. Tucking the leather-bound menu under his arm, he surveyed the cheese platter, the champagne bucket, the crystal flutes and the box of condoms. He could do this. He'd seen a movie where the guy carried flutes without using his hands—except he wouldn't make the mistake the guy had.

He shoved a flute in each of his hip pockets. Then he tucked the condom box under one arm, grabbed the champagne bucket and picked up the cheese tray.

When he walked into the bedroom with all of it, she laughed. "That's awesome, but where are the flutes?"

He turned to show her.

"Oh, my God! Like in *Sabrina*."

"That's the one. I just have to remember not to sit down."

"I love that movie. Both the original and the re-make."

"Me, too." He set the ice bucket on the nightstand and put the cheese platter on the bed. After placing the box of condoms on the nightstand, he handed her the menu before pulling the flutes out of his back pockets. "Safe. Want some champagne?"

"I'd love some." She studied the menu, but did not, however, pick up any of the cheese.

He peeled the foil off the champagne bottle. "Grab a flute, will you? I don't know if this will foam or not."

"Okay." She laid down the menu and picked up one of the glasses. "Maybe we should do this in the bathroom."

He glanced at her. Old habits were hard to break, but he had an inspiration on how to confront this one and have fun doing it. At least he'd have fun. "I have a better idea. Lie down while you're holding the glass."

"Lie down?"

"Yeah." He cautiously twisted the metal wire holding the cork in place. Sometimes the bottles blew once that was gone. He'd rather this one didn't.

"If you say so." She moved the cheese platter to the other side of the bed and stretched out. "Where should I hold it?"

"Oh, let's see." Before he finished taking off the wire, he guided her hand until the flute was poised about three inches above her navel. "That should do it."

"I think I know where this is headed."

"Too obvious?"

"If you want to drip champagne on me you could do it after you've poured it."

"But then there's no adventure." He took off the wire and the cork stayed put. Using the small towel the hotel had provided, he placed it over the cork and put one knee on the bed so he could open the bottle close to where she held the glass.

"If you get the sheets soaked you're sleeping on this side."

"I don't know about you, but I don't plan to do much sleeping tonight." To his intense disappointment, the cork popped out and he didn't get a drop of champagne on her luscious body. He'd have to be a little sloppy when he poured it, then.

Tossing the towel and cork aside, he leaned down and carefully poured champagne into the flute. He kept pouring.

"Zach, that's enough. Zach!" she yelped as the

bubbly liquid trickled over the top of the glass and spilled onto her silky skin. "I *knew* you would do this. I knew it."

"And you were right! Here, let me have that glass before you spill all over yourself."

"Very funny. This champagne is cold, Zach. Extremely cold."

"Let's see if I can warm you up." After setting down her glass on the nightstand, he climbed onto the bed.

"I hope you're getting a charge out of this."

"I am. So will you." He began to lick the champagne where it had pooled in her navel.

"That's…different."

"I'm just getting started." He licked his way up to her breasts. "Darn, no champagne. Let me fix that." He picked up the flute and dribbled some onto her.

She gasped. "Still cold."

"I'm working on that." He licked away the little trails of liquid. A subtle change in her breathing told him she was starting to get into this.

Picking up the glass again, he took a sip of champagne and held it on his tongue while he cupped her breast. Slowly he drew her nipple into his mouth and began to suck until the bubbles danced against her sensitive skin.

"Oh!" She quivered in reaction.

Swallowing the champagne, he took another small sip and treated her other nipple to the same experience. As he sucked, he reached between her thighs. She must like this, if her slick heat was any indication. And he'd saved the best for last.

Taking in a last mouthful, he slid down between

her thighs. She knew what he was up to, because she opened to him with a little moan of welcome. Sliding his hands under her bottom, he lifted her to the angle he needed. He lost some of the champagne in his quest but he still had enough to create a fizzy sensation at that tender spot guaranteed to bring her to the edge.

As the bubbles worked their magic, he pushed two fingers deep and stroked her, lazily at first. As she caught fire, he picked up the pace. Within seconds she arched into his caress with a wild cry and the taste of her climax mingled with the tang of champagne.

She sank back to the mattress and murmured a soft oath.

After kissing his way back up her slightly sticky body, he gazed into her flushed face. "Is there a problem?"

Her breathing was still ragged. "You bet there is."

"You didn't enjoy that?"

"You know I did."

"Then what's the matter?"

"I'll never be able to drink champagne again without remembering this."

"Oh." He smiled. "Sorry."

"No, you're not."

"You're right, I'm not. I'm human. I want to leave you with some indelible memories. So shoot me."

"I'll find a way to get you back. I'll make sure I leave you with some indelible memories, too."

He looked into her green eyes and knew they'd haunt him long after she was gone. "Trust me, you already have."

6

ON SOME LEVEL Jeannette knew they were playing a dangerous game that could end in emotional disaster. If she'd had any sense, she'd have rejected his idea of one spectacular night together. But she hadn't been able to make herself do the sensible thing.

She'd spent her life being sensible, until the incident with Drake. Letting herself be sucked into that drama had taught her that she was itching to live a far less ordered life. But she wasn't willing to repeat the kind of behavior that had wrecked long-standing friendships. From now on she'd consider whether her choices would impact others.

Spending the night at this hotel affected only two people—herself and Zach. Apparently he was ready to teach her how to be less sensible, as evidenced by the adventure with champagne. She tingled with anticipation as she imagined what other surprises he had in store.

Their order of club sandwiches and fries arrived quickly. She'd overridden Zach's suggestion that they choose a gourmet dinner with the argument that it would take longer to prepare. He'd grumbled a bit but once she'd agreed to eat the meal in bed, he'd been fine with it.

She'd put on the complimentary hotel bathrobe while they waited for the bellman to bring a dinner cart. The bellman left the cart in the living room because Jeannette hadn't wanted to advertise that they would eat in bed.

Zach began unbuttoning his shirt. "No reason for me to stay dressed anymore, right?"

"Um, yes, there is." She watched the shirt come off and gulped. "Are you planning to eat naked?" He hadn't been kidding about the muscles he'd developed shoveling out stalls.

"Why not? Aren't you?"

"I hadn't decided."

"That's part of the fun of eating in bed. Then if we take a notion, we don't have to fool with clothes." He sat on the nearest upholstered chair and pulled off his socks, which made his powerful biceps flex.

"Take a notion? That sounds like cowboy talk." Jeannette longed to touch him. She wanted to lick, rub and caress every inch of his muscled torso.

"I know." He grinned. "It's not enough to wear the clothes. You gotta talk the talk." He stood and casually unbuttoned his jeans.

She, on the other hand, was becoming more agitated by the second. She took a steadying breath. "Zach, I think we really need to eat these sandwiches."

"I was planning on it." His zipper rasped.

"It may have escaped your notice, but I've been naked practically since we arrived in this suite. You've probably become used to the idea."

"I wouldn't say I'm *used* to it. Looking at you still gets me hot."

"Exactly, but maybe not as fiercely as when I first stripped. You, on the other hand, have been mostly clothed."

"I'm about to remedy that." He started to shove both jeans and briefs down.

"Wait."

"Wait?"

"I don't think you took my meaning. If you shuck those clothes, I can't be responsible for my actions."

A slow grin spread across his handsome face. "I do like the sound of that."

"But I really need to eat some dinner."

"Oh. So you're trying to tell me that the sight of my naked body will be so arousing that you won't be able to concentrate on your meal?"

"I am saying that, yes."

"Huh." He seemed quite pleased with the thought. "Do you need me to put my shirt back on?"

"That's not necessary." And it would be a crime against nature. Now that she'd seen him without it, she thought he should make going shirtless a permanent wardrobe choice. "But if you could leave your jeans on until we finish the meal, I'd be very grateful."

"I can do that." He zipped up and fastened the button at his waist. "Better?"

"Yes."

"I guess I thought, since you'd already been up close and personal with what's inside these jeans, it wouldn't matter whether I wore them or not."

"It matters."

"Okay, then. Ready to retire to the bedroom?"

"Yes, but I have another request."

"If you want to leave your bathrobe on, that's fine. I understand your point about needing food."

"I think we also need a distraction. Let's see what movies are available."

He gazed at her. "So you want to sit in bed eating sandwiches and watching movies? Like we're roommates hanging out together?"

"At least until we finish the meal."

"Are you a fast eater?"

"Zach!"

"Well, you said you're a power shopper, so it's a reasonable question."

"I'm not goin' to rush through dinner so we can have sex." At least not on purpose. But she really did want to get her hands on that lovely torso of his. She wanted to run her fingers through the chest hair that swirled around his nipples and formed a sexy line that disappeared under his waistband. After the meal was over, he could take off those jeans, too. And then she'd—

"Jeannette?"

"What?" She felt her cheeks heat. She'd been caught ogling.

"I asked what kind of movie you wanted to watch."

"Oh, a comedy."

"Then let's see what's on." He walked to the desk, grabbed a movie guide and flipped through it. "Would you believe the *Sabrina* remake is on right now?"

"Then let's watch that."

He handed her the movie guide. "You're in charge of that. I'll bring in the cart."

"I know this isn't what you envisioned, but—"

"Don't worry about it. My little fantasy will come later. I ordered us chocolate mousse for dessert."

"You didn't tell me that."

"My little surprise."

And that was exactly why she needed to spend the night with this man. He was determined to blast her right out of her comfort zone. "I suppose you want to eat that in bed, too."

"And off each other."

He must be having an effect on her, because she was ready to forget about their club sandwiches and go straight to dessert. But she'd requested a movie with dinner. After consulting the movie guide, she turned on the huge flat screen in the bedroom and clicked through the offerings until she found the listing for *Sabrina*.

If she were to apply the story line to her situation with Zach, she'd have to reverse the roles. She was more of a nose-to-the-grindstone type, while Zach was the impulsive one, at least now that he'd stopped practicing law to become a cowboy.

She still struggled with the idea that he'd abandoned his profession. Society desperately needed lawyers who weren't focused on earning big fees and winning high-profile cases. He could be as low-key and altruistic as he wanted, but to deprive the world of his ability as a principled lawyer—that seemed wrong.

"Got it cued up?"

"I do."

"I'll put the cart on my side of the bed." He started around to the far side.

"Hold it. That's the part that wasn't baptized with

champagne. I'll take that side and you can have the other one."

He shrugged and steered the cart back around to the other side. "I'm good with either. I don't mind a few champagne splatters. Speaking of that, do you want more?"

"How do you mean that, exactly?"

His sexy mouth lifted at the corners. "How do you want me to mean it? You might complain about spills, but I seem to recall that you had a really good time with the bubbly."

He would have to mention that episode, which reminded her of how his mouth had felt when he... She called a halt to those erotic thoughts. If she started remembering all the pleasure he'd given her since they'd checked into this suite, she would die of starvation. She'd die happy, but still...a woman could not live on sex alone.

She gazed at this arousing, imaginative, challenging man. He would never let her get away with being stuffy and boring. He'd bring out the vixen in her. He'd awaken the rebel who wasn't satisfied with the status quo even when she pretended to be coloring inside the lines.

She faced him across the wide expanse of the king-size mattress. "I had a great time with you and the bubbly, as we established earlier. I have a feelin' that before the meal is over, you'll have changed my relationship with chocolate mousse, too."

"It's my sincerest wish."

"I figured as much. For now, though, I'd like some champagne in a glass, please."

"I can do that."

He was as good as his word. Once they were settled on the bed, he handed her a glass of champagne without dribbling any on her. It wouldn't have worked, anyway, because she'd decided to keep the bathrobe on while they ate.

"Aren't you warm in that bulky thing?" He sounded disappointed that she was so covered up.

"Not really." She wasn't warm. She was hot, and not because the room temperature was too high. Every time she glanced at him propped against a mound of pillows, a shirtless fantasy man if she'd ever seen one, she wanted to jump his bones.

She considered asking him to put his shirt back on after all, but he looked so comfy. And so tanned. He must have spent part of his time outdoors soaking up the Wyoming sunshine. Dear God, he was gorgeous. She forced herself to look away before she ruined the program she'd been so committed to.

They each balanced their plates on their laps as they watched the movie. She noticed they laughed in the same places. When Greg Kinnear sat on the glasses tucked in his back pocket, they looked at each other and grinned.

"You know what?" Zach kept his attention on the screen as he picked up a fry from his plate.

"What?"

"This is fun." He popped the fry in his mouth.

"I think so, too." She watched him while pretending she wasn't. He was absorbed in the movie.

"I mean, really fun. I got so tired of the Hollywood scene that I didn't want to watch movies anymore. And I love movies. It's the reason I got into entertainment law in the first place."

Her heart twisted when she thought of his broken dreams. He must have imagined that working in Hollywood as a lawyer would make him happy. For some people, it might, but it seemed he wasn't suited to the frenetic pace or the pressure to make piles of money. "Then I'm glad we're doing this."

"Me, too. But just so you know, I'm still thinking about you over there naked under your bathrobe. That might be why this is so fun. It's like an X-rated version of a sleepover."

"I like that."

"So do I." He continued to watch the movie and eat his fries. When he was finished and had set his plate on the nightstand, he spoke again. "Is it okay if we pause the movie for a minute? This next part is great but I wanted to say something that's been on my mind."

"Sure." She put her empty plate on the nightstand, too, picked up the remote and clicked the pause button before turning to him. "What?"

"I've been thinking about the things you said earlier, about having women friends I loved but didn't sleep with. I'm not sure I've had close women friends, period. If I slept with them, sex was the focus, not friendship."

"That's too bad."

"It is, I guess, but I'm still not sure the concept works, at least for a man. There's always a sexual component. I mean, you had these two great guys as friends, but look what happened."

She sighed. "I know. Point taken."

"Maybe now you can be friends with them, but will you really be that close? Regan has a fiancée, and Drake moved in with Tracy. You may always be friends with those guys, but best buds? I'm not so sure."

"You're right, of course. Lily is great, and I'm sure Tracy is cool with me, too, but…yeah. It won't be the same. Lily will be Regan's best friend and Tracy will be Drake's. That's the way it should be. I'll fit in a different category of friend—still close, but not as close."

"That's where I was going with this. I never thought about it before, but that's what has been missing from every relationship I've had with a woman. We were lovers, but we weren't necessarily friends. And that was my fault."

She couldn't let him shoulder the blame. "I doubt it was entirely your fault. Each person has a part in building—"

"No, it was my fault, and I'll tell you why. We never did stuff like this." He swept a hand around the room.

"Sure you did. You obviously are used to sharing a meal in bed with a woman."

"But not while we were watching TV. Do you see the difference? We're just sitting here and watching something instead of turning the meal into a sexual adventure. We found a movie we both liked and it's been fun watching it together, right?"

"It has, but I can't believe you didn't watch movies with the women in your life."

"Of course I did, but hardly ever for the pure fun of it. We knew too much about the industry, so we'd fall into the trap of criticizing this or that, and the joy would seep right out of the experience. Bad, bad habit."

"And not much fun, really."

"Not much." He met her gaze. "And another thing. What we're doing right now, talking about things that matter. I never used to do that with them."

"Why not?"

"I don't know. Maybe…hell, it's obvious, isn't it? I couldn't bitch about my frustrations with my job, because that would be a total buzzkill and destroy my precious image. So I clammed up about the one thing that was driving me nuts."

"And they didn't get to see the real you."

"Right." He stared at her, his gray eyes thoughtful. "And now that you say that, I'll bet I didn't get to see the real them, either. Lots of people wear masks in Hollywood. I did. I was the successful lawyer who drove a Lamborghini."

"Pricey car."

"No kidding. If you think that truck oozes testosterone, you should have seen my black Lamborghini. If I'd really fixed myself, I would have bought a used pickup. Maybe a faded brown one."

She reached over and stroked his cheek. "Don't be so hard on yourself, Zach. It's a beautiful truck. You don't have to deny yourself all the perks."

"But it's impractical as hell." He caught her hand and pressed a kiss into her palm. Then he laced his fingers through hers. "If you're going to drive on ranch roads, you need a truck the color of dirt."

"That's not you, either. You have too much energy to drive a truck the color of dirt."

"Jack has a red truck. It doesn't show the dirt nearly as much as mine." He gazed at her. "And speaking of the ranch, I didn't think through this hotel stay very well."

"I don't know." She smiled at him. "I think it's worked out very well."

"Up to now, you bet. But I'm afraid I fell back into my old way of thinking once I booked a luxury hotel. I'm no longer a lawyer who can reschedule his morning appointments. I'm a ranch hand, and I have to be back on the job at dawn."

"Right." She glanced at the time on the bedside clock and discovered it was past midnight. "And we're an hour away from Shoshone."

He nodded. "Besides that, I'll need to factor in dropping you at the B and B."

"What you're saying is that we don't have much more time here."

"Sadly, no."

"Zach, I just thought of something. I can take a nap at the Bunk and Grub, but you have to work. When will you sleep?"

"I get off at two tomorrow, so I can grab a quick nap before the party at five."

"That doesn't seem like enough time."

He grinned. "Ask me if I care."

"I care. Let's leave now so you can grab at least an hour or two before you have to head to work."

"Let's not." He reached over and loosened the belt of her robe.

Her heart started thudding faster. "Are you still fixated on that chocolate mousse?"

"Oddly enough, I'm not. I'm more in the mood for good, old-fashioned sex." He looked into her eyes. "Would that be okay with you?"

Her breath caught. The emotion in his gaze matched the warmth she was feeling. It was no longer simply lust between them. Something more was going on. Considering that fact, playing around with chocolate mousse might be a safer option than face-to-face lovemaking.

Funny how the issue of stepping out of her comfort zone had just shifted to include missionary-position sex with a man who was supposed to be essentially a one-night stand. "Yes," she said. "Totally okay with me."

7

ZACH LEFT THE bed so he could get out of the rest of his clothes. If he'd started this meal the way he'd intended, he wouldn't have to do that, but if he'd started the meal naked, they would have been rolling around in that bed in no time. Wearing the jeans had been a good thing, a lesson in postponing sex so he could actually get to know a woman. And himself.

The more he got to know Jeannette, the more he chafed against their abbreviated time together. But he'd worry about that later. At the moment he had no worries whatsoever, because she was waiting for him in that big bed.

He rolled on a condom before he joined her there, because he wouldn't be playing any games this time. Games were fun when you had all the time in the world, but he and Jeannette didn't. Despite having fun doing it on the floor and the various oral variations that had followed, he secretly loved this way the best.

As he climbed back into bed and moved between her thighs, he realized that he'd denied himself this favorite position most of the time. He'd been afraid his partners would find it unimaginative and boring. Luckily Jeannette didn't look bored.

Her green eyes were bright as she slid both hands up his chest and around his neck. "Welcome."

"You don't think this is clichéd?"

Her laughter was breathless. "You *have* been in Hollywood too long."

"Yeah." He would get down to business in a minute. First he wanted to remain braced above her so he could watch her skin flush as the tip of his cock nudged her entrance.

"Mmm." She lifted her hips and took him in a fraction more.

Adrenaline shot through him, tempting him to accept her unspoken invitation to thrust deep. But he was still enjoying his view. Her breasts quivered with every rapid breath she took and her nipples were tight buds of arousal. "I'd almost forgotten how much I like having sex like this."

"I do, too." She kneaded his shoulders. "I like watching your eyes change color."

"They do?" No one had ever told him that.

"Uh-huh. Light to dark."

He pushed in farther. "So do yours."

"Not…surprised." She flattened her hands against his chest. "You feel good."

"Where?"

"Here." She rubbed his pecs.

"Here?" He rotated his hips.

Her eyes flashed green fire. Then she clutched his hips, wrapped her legs around his and lifted up, taking him all the way. *"There."*

If he'd had any breath left, he would have laughed,

but she'd taken it all away with that feisty move. If he'd thought he was in control, she'd just proved him wrong. He didn't care. He was exactly where he wanted to be, buried to the hilt in her warmth.

Settling down on his forearms, he gazed into her eyes and gulped in air. "Nice move."

"You were dawdlin'."

"My apologies." He was securely anchored and he loved the feeling, but he thought they both might benefit from a looser situation. "Gonna let me move?"

She smiled. "Only if you promise to be nice."

He leaned down, his mouth hovering over hers. "What's nice?"

"You know perfectly well."

He touched his mouth to hers and slid his tongue inside. After stroking back and forth a few times, he lifted his head. "Like that?"

"You're gettin' the idea, cowboy."

"Then ease up so I can be nice where it counts."

She relaxed her grip but kept her legs wrapped around his.

Propping himself up a little more so he could watch her expression, he began a slow rhythm. "How's that?"

"It'll do."

God, but she made him smile. The heat in her gaze told him that she liked it better than she was letting on, but he loved her saucy attitude. Here he'd been worried that missionary-position sex would be a cliché.

He doubted that sex would ever be a cliché when he made love to Jeannette. They brought out the playfulness in each other. Teasing her and being teased back was as natural as breathing.

And speaking of breathing, hers was getting a little

rapid, as if she might be excited. Imagine that. Shifting his angle, he drove in deeper, with a slightly faster pace. "Like that?"

"For…the time bein'…" Her little whimper gave her away.

"I think you're getting hot." He sure as hell was. The blood rushed in his ears and his cock wanted more, and faster yet. So he gave his bad boy what it longed for, and thrust in time with a wild, primitive beat.

Her lips parted and her gaze took on the intensity of her looming orgasm. He watched avidly as her expression signaled that her moment was near. Oh, yeah. This was why he loved this position.

"I think you're gonna come," he murmured softly. He stroked swiftly, his attention on her eyes. "You're gonna come right…*now*." He pushed deep and she closed her eyes and arched upward with a helpless cry of surrender. It was the sweetest sound, the greatest gift.

With a groan, he unleashed the climax he'd barely been able to contain. Gasping, he pulsed within her and thanked his lucky stars that this woman had entered his life. If he had his way, it would be for more than one night.

When his breathing had slowed, he kissed her softly. "Beautiful." For him that was a global statement that covered her and the sex they'd just shared.

"It was." Her eyes fluttered open. "But now we should probably—"

"In a little bit. Don't go anywhere. I'll be right back." Reluctantly he eased away from her, sat up and swung his feet to the floor.

"But I should get up, too." She pushed herself to a sitting position.

"Not yet. Please." He stood and turned to her. "Just stay there, okay?"

She hesitated before sliding back down. "All right."

"Great." He hurried into the bathroom while he wondered how in hell he could avoid the separation that was about to happen. He'd see what they might be able to work out, because he wasn't ready for this to be over.

When he came back into the room, she was lying on her side, her head propped on a pillow as she gazed at him. He climbed in and mirrored her position. "I can't speak for you, but I'm not ready to end this."

She sighed. "Neither am I, but I don't know what else to do. I'm not going to risk sneakin' you up to my room at the Bunk and Grub."

"You could stay in my Airstream." He figured she'd say no, but he had to put it out there.

She regarded him silently for several long seconds. "That wouldn't do my reputation any good."

"Probably not." He couldn't very well deny it. "Okay, forget that idea. But I just…" He cupped her cheek. "I just hate to think you'll be so close, and yet so far."

"I know. I'll be thinkin' of you the whole time."

"Same here."

She sighed again. "And we'll both be miserable."

"I'll try not to be, but yeah, I'll pretty much hate seeing you at the party and knowing I can't be with you after it's over."

"Come to think of it, my reputation isn't in very good shape as it is."

Maybe all wasn't lost, then, but a sense of fairness made him remind her of her original goal. "I thought you were trying to fix that."

She pressed his hand against her cheek. "I was, until we had this time together. The people that matter most to me, Regan and Drake, won't care if I spend the rest of the weekend with you. As for everybody else, their good opinion doesn't seem so important if you and I have to suffer in order to earn it."

"Are you sure about this? I don't want to let you in for more of what you've been through."

She gazed at him. "When I weigh that against us having more time together, their disapproval doesn't matter so much anymore."

"Ah, Jeannette." He gathered her close and combed his fingers through her hair. "I'm trying not to think of how selfish I'm being by wanting to take you back with me."

"But I want to go." She hugged him tight. "I'm dyin' of curiosity about that solar shower."

Laughing, he rolled her to her back. "You'll love it. We'll take a shower together when I come back from work, before we get dressed for the party."

"Which I now have a date for, right?"

"You most certainly do."

"We should get started back, then, so we can pick up my stuff and my car before you have to go to work."

"We will." He reached for a condom on the nightstand. "But first we need one for the road."

AN HOUR LATER, they were headed back to Shoshone, and he was glad he'd only had a few drops of champagne licked from Jeannette's sweet body. His head was clear and his imagination was busily concocting scenarios of what would happen when they reached his campsite. Jeannette seemed determined that he'd get an hour or so of sleep, but he doubted it. Traffic was light, which allowed him to jack up his speed.

"You should sleep on the way home," he told her.

"Not on your life. We need some tunes, is what we need." She leaned over and switched on the radio. His favorite classic rock station came on with a number by Billy Joel. "Do you mean to tell me you don't have a country station locked in to go with your big bad truck?"

"Sorry. If you want country, you can search around and find some."

"What if I like this?"

He glanced over at her. "Then I guess we're good." Were they ever. Each similarity they discovered underlined how good they would be together. He wondered if she'd noticed that. "I figured you'd like the newer stuff."

"I like some of it, but my parents were older when they had me, so they played this kind of music all the time. I grew up on it."

"So did I, although my parents weren't terribly old when they had me. If you went to school with Regan and Drake, you must be what, thirty?"

"A lady doesn't discuss her age."

"If you won't discuss it, I'll have to conclude that you went back to college after working several dead-end jobs and you're now pushing forty."

"I am not!"

"Okay, I'll go first. I'm thirty-six." When he was

with her, though, he felt like a teenager with his first crush.

"That old, huh?"

"That old. When I graduated from law school, you were a wet-behind-the-ears freshman in college. It's a wonder we connect at all."

"Sarcasm."

"Do you think?"

"In actuality, a thirty-six-year-old man is about right for a thirty-year-old woman. Women mature faster than men."

He decided to ignore that comment. "So you admit to being thirty?"

"I do. I was supposed to be married by now. I was on track for it, too."

"If you were supposed to be married by now, what about me? I'm way past the age when I should have found the perfect woman and settled down."

"Come to think of it, you are old to never have been married. Are you divorced?"

"Nope."

"Why not?"

He laughed. "Because I didn't get married. It's kind of hard to get a divorce from a wife you've never had."

"I said that wrong. Let's try that again. Why haven't you ever been married?"

"Damn, now you sound like my mother. She's been pestering me for years about that."

"And what do you tell her?"

He focused on the white dividing line rolling past. "I tell her the same thing I'll tell you. I haven't found the right person." A small voice whispered that he might have found her now, but that was a ridiculously premature idea. "I did get engaged once, but we both figured out it wouldn't work and broke up."

"Smart. Regan and I should have done that. But on the other hand, if we had, I never would have met you. I'm glad for whatever circumstances brought us together."

"Me, too." More than she'd ever know, probably. "I take it your parents were pushing you to get married, too. Expecting you to give them grandkids and all that."

"Get married, yes. That's generally what Southern girls are supposed to do. I don't think they were particularly eager for grandchildren, though. They didn't intend to have me in the first place."

"Oh."

She sighed. "Blame the late hour. I didn't mean to blurt that out. Please don't think I dwell on it, or think of myself as some kind of mistake. Once they had me, they were very proud of me and what I accomplished."

"As well they should be." But his heart ached for her. No wonder she'd tried to be Miss Perfect all her life. She'd been trying to justify her right to exist.

He had the crazy urge to coax her away from Virginia and what sounded like a toxic situation. Maybe she wasn't all that happy at work. "Tell me about your job."

She seemed grateful for a change of subject. "It's terrific. My firm has a lot of clients who own and race Thoroughbreds. Sale contracts get complicated, especially for a foal that might go on to be a Derby winner. Everyone's always looking for the next Triple Crown hopeful. Very high-pressure, but I love it."

"And the horses can't show up drunk or stoned. That would be a plus."

She laughed. "Some of the owners might, though. Wherever there's money, there's excess. I'm sure I don't have to tell you that."

"Sure don't."

"I'm about to make partner." She said it softly, but with a touch of pride.

"No kidding? That's great!" Not for him, obviously. His tentative idea that she might consider moving to Jackson Hole and open a practice seemed doomed from the start.

If she'd worked her tail off for this firm and was about to be offered a partnership, she wouldn't want to give that up without a really good reason. He was willing to try to provide her with a reason, but that was a tall order, even though he'd stretched their one-night-stand into a three-day affair. A long-distance relationship was an option, but he'd never been a fan of those. He'd seen too many Hollywood couples break up because they didn't spend enough time together.

"My folks are happy about the partnership."

"I'll bet." Yeah, they would be. They might have suffered through botched wedding plans, but they could take solace in their daughter's professional success. Zach didn't think he'd like them very much.

Even if they hadn't planned to have Jeannette, why tell her so? Only selfishness, insensitivity or both would motivate a parent to blab something like that to a kid. He didn't have much patience with either, especially when he witnessed the fallout—a woman who thought she had to do everything just right.

Then "Jailhouse Rock" came on, and Jeannette

started singing along. He thought that was so cute that he joined in, and soon the two of them were belting out the song at the top of their lungs. They both made love better than they sang, but it didn't matter. Cruising down the highway in the wee hours of the morning, singing along with Elvis, he couldn't remember when he'd ever been happier.

She knew the Buddy Holly song that came on next, too, and they ended up singing like fools for the rest of the trip. He'd made the drive from Shoshone to Jackson several times in the month he'd lived here, but it had never seemed as short as it did tonight. Logically he should be exhausted, but being with Jeannette gave him a second wind.

The streets of Shoshone were deserted at this hour, but when Zach came to the intersection, the light turned red. "It always does this. Jack says Elmer Crookshanks, the guy with the gas station on the corner, has a sensor so you have to stop and look over at his station."

"You could run it."

"I could, but Elmer used to have a traffic camera hooked up, too. Jack swears he made him take it down, but I've heard others say it's still running. Might as well sit here until it turns green."

"This is a quirky little town." She looked over at the Spirits and Spurs. The neon sign depicting a cowboy on a bucking bronco had been turned off. "That bar looks like fun."

"Supposedly it's haunted. That's why Josie calls it the Spirits and Spurs. Kind of an inside joke."

"I met Josie today while we were working in the kitchen. Pretty lady, long blond braid."

"That's her."

"I didn't realize she owns the local bar."

"Didn't Regan or Drake give you a cheat sheet?"

"Like I said, they've both been involved with the new women in their lives, and I'm fine with that. I'll muddle through."

"You're not going to have to muddle anymore. Before we go to the party, I'll give you a rundown."

"That would be great." She paused. "We won't be in danger of upstaging Regan and Lily, will we? I'd never want to do that."

"I'll clue Jack in before I leave work so he can pass the word around. And we'll keep a low profile." He wasn't sure if that would work considering the gossip that had been swirling before. That gossip would erupt when people found out she'd left the Bunk and Grub to stay with him. But he'd do his damnedest. Her major concern might be for Regan and Lily, but his first concern was for her.

One dim light shone from a front window of the Victorian house that Pam Mulholland had turned into a bed-and-breakfast. Jeannette had him wait while she went in and quickly packed her things and left a note at the reception desk. She didn't waste time. She was in and out with no visible signs that anyone had heard her.

He watched her sling her suitcase in the backseat of her rental car. Then he pulled forward so she could follow him out of the small parking lot. From the moment she'd left the cab of his truck, he'd missed her.

Once she was behind him, he took the road out of town toward the ranch. She'd driven it before, but he kept tabs on his rearview mirror, anyway, to make sure her headlights were reflected there. His protective instincts had developed without him realizing it. Now, they weren't together and he had to think about whether she was safe back there.

The dirt road into the ranch property had been washboard-rough ever since he'd arrived a month ago. The family had an ongoing debate about it, with Jack insisting it stay that way because his dad had intended to make visiting difficult. His two brothers believed that customers for the registered Paints the Chances sold would appreciate a paved entrance to the property.

Zach's truck had no problem with the road, but he winced as Jeannette's rental car bounced around. He went slowly, even though he was eager to get her ensconced in the Airstream. They drove past the massive ranch house, a two-story log structure with a central section and two wings set at an angle, like arms reaching out.

The house was dark, the ranch buildings lit with a few dusk-to-dawn lamps. Otherwise the place was quiet. In a couple of hours, though, as the sun peeked over the horizon, the hustle and bustle would begin.

Normally Zach looked forward to that time of day, but maybe he could be forgiven if he'd rather stay in the Airstream with Jeannette this morning. He wouldn't do it, though. Once she was tucked into bed, he'd head back to the ranch to work his shift.

The road to his campsite was filled with even more ruts. Maybe he should have told her to park at the ranch and then join him in his truck, but her car would create more gossip. This was better. They'd be tucked away, out of sight and maybe out of mind.

He didn't really believe that, but at least he'd be on hand to shield her from whatever came her way. Maybe nothing would. The Last Chance had been established as a place where people and animals really could have one last chance to set things right. Jeannette had come to Jackson Hole for that very purpose.

At last he turned on a smaller dirt road and within minutes saw the silver gleam of his trailer in the moonlight. He parked and hopped out so he could guide her to a parking spot where the ground was firm.

She pulled in, shut off the motor and got out of the car. "It's so quiet. But it smells great, like Christmas trees. Wait, I can hear the water. That's the stream, right?"

"That's the stream." He pulled her close because he couldn't help himself. He wanted to surround her with whatever security he could provide.

An owl hooted, and she shivered. "I should warn you that I've never camped before."

"That's okay. You'll love it." He had no basis for saying that, and maybe it was wishful thinking on his part.

"Will you stay until it gets light?"

"Yes." He could tell she was nervous, but she would get over it. He'd make love to her in his double bed under the curved roof of his Airstream with the windows open so they could hear the night sounds while they enjoyed each other.

He wanted her to fall in love with the woods the way he had. He couldn't explain why that was so important to him. He only knew that it was.

8

WHEN JEANNETTE HAD agreed to this plan, she'd only thought about being with Zach in his cozy little trailer. She'd thought about the solar shower, mostly in terms of watching him take one. She hadn't thought about the bears.

She didn't want to mention them now, either, and look like a total wuss. At least Zach would stay until the sun started to rise. He had to be at work by dawn, but that was a flexible description. He wasn't punching a time clock.

Although she wasn't clear on bear behavior, she thought they were mostly nocturnal. Even if they weren't, a bear would be much scarier in the dark than in broad daylight. She could see a bear coming when the sun was out, and she had her phone.

Zach continued to hold her close, probably because she was still shivering a little. "Ready to check out the Airstream?"

"Yep."

He released her. "I'll unlock the tailgate so you can haul the shopping bags in. I'll handle your suitcase."

"Okay." It wasn't cold at all, and moonlight lit up the clearing pretty well. She shouldn't be scared, but as she followed him to the back of the truck, she started to shiver again. "How's the phone reception out here?"

"Not that great. It's sporadic on the ranch property." He pulled the tailgate down. "Sometimes it's great and sometimes not. This area is kind of a dead spot. If you need to make a call, your best bet is to try when you're up at the house."

Crap. "Oh, well. Not important."

He unhooked the bungee cord holding the two shopping bags and handed both of them to her. Then he closed the tailgate with a clang. "Do you need to make a call?"

"Not right now." She'd been listening intently for the sound of pine needles crunching under heavy paws. She had no idea what kind of noise an approaching bear would make, but if she heard any shuffling or crunching, she was diving into Zach's truck. It seemed more bear-proof than her flimsy rental car.

"You could try texting if you want to reach your assistant. That might work."

"Sure. I'll do that later." She'd let him think that contacting Erin was the only reason she'd need a phone out here. Something rustled in the wild bushes growing among the trees. She froze. "Wh-what was that?"

"I don't know." He walked toward her car, obviously unconcerned. "Maybe a raccoon. Maybe a skunk."

"A *skunk?*" She mostly didn't want to be eaten by

a bear, but she had no interest in being sprayed by a skunk, either. "Let's get inside."

"Most things around here won't bother you if you don't mess with them." He pulled her suitcase out of the backseat and closed the door. Then he held out his hand. "Come on. Check out the silver bullet."

"Is that its name?" She felt better the minute he laced his strong fingers through hers.

"Not this one, specifically. People call Airstreams silver bullets for obvious reasons."

"It sure is shiny."

"It was a lot shinier before I pulled it over those dirt roads. Fortunately we had some rain and that washed it down some."

She heard the pride in his voice and guessed that he was excited to show off his trailer. "Is it old? I know these used to be popular a long time ago."

"It's new. I thought about buying a restored one, but I'm a beginner at this RV thing and I needed a manual and a warranty. My grandparents had one of these, and I used to love going on road trips with them, so it's all about the nostalgia." He squeezed her hand and let go. "Need to get my keys out."

"Sure." She looked around as he went up the small steps and unlocked the door, but whatever had rustled before wasn't doing it anymore. She couldn't get over the feeling that unseen eyes were watching her, though. Made sense. She was in the wilds with wild creatures. Of course they'd be watching.

Zach walked into the trailer, set down her bag and flicked a light switch.

She didn't wait for an invitation to follow him. She

stayed right on his heels. Whatever had rustled in the bushes could be right on *her* heels for all she knew.

He turned and bumped into her. "Oops. Sorry. Didn't realize you were so close. So this is… Oh, hey, did you hear that?"

"What?" Shopping bags held in front of her as some kind of barrier, she whirled to face the door in case that bushes-rustling animal was climbing the steps. She saw nothing in the light spilling out the door.

"Be real quiet. Maybe we'll hear it again."

Although she had a strong urge to close that door, she didn't. She also tried to be quiet, but her heart pounded loud enough to drown out anything they might be listening for. She'd have to count on Zach to be her ears right now. "Hear what?" she whispered.

"Wolves."

She swallowed a little whimper of anxiety. "Are they close?" She knew logically a wolf wasn't any danger to people, but still. If one walked up those steps and looked her in the eye, she'd have trouble being calm about it. She was used to horse farms that hadn't seen a bear or a wolf in generations.

"Not very. Maybe they won't howl again. Go ahead and make yourself at home."

"Okay." She set her shopping bags on either side of her and tried not to rattle them too loud.

Then the sound came again. Now she recognized it as a howl, and every hair on her body stood on end.

"Did you hear that?" Zach's low voice vibrated with excitement.

"Yes." Another howl from a different direction seemed to answer the one that had come before it.

"What a treat. Howling wolves on your first night." Zach wrapped his arms around her waist and pulled her back against his solid warmth.

The first wolf howled again.

"They're talking," he murmured.

"About what?" Now that Zach had both arms around her and she knew a wolf wouldn't come charging in the door, she relaxed a little. Their calls to each other off in the distance were kind of cool. If the wolves stayed there, they could make as much noise as they wanted.

"Possibly they're announcing their presence to keep one pack from encroaching on another pack's territory."

"How do they know where the boundaries are?"

"The alpha males mark their territory by peeing on trees and rocks."

"Oh."

"They're fascinating creatures. Loyal, brave, smart. I've always loved them."

"I can tell." The longer they stood there listening to the wolves howl with her backside pressed up against his groin, the more she became aware of his interest in other subjects besides wolves.

Sliding both hands up to cup her breasts, he leaned down and nuzzled behind her ear. "I've never had a pretty lady in my arms while the wolves howled. I think it's bringing out the beast in me."

"Is that so?" Camping in the woods might have some advantages—she hadn't considered that it might awaken his inner alpha male. The howling wolves had stirred her up some, too, especially when she'd realized he was getting hard.

But she felt some responsibility for seeing that he rested for the hour or so before he had to leave. She captured his hands and held them still. "You really should take a quick nap."

"No, thanks." Escaping her grip easily, he drew back her collar and nipped the sensitive skin of her neck.

It didn't hurt, but it sure as heck turned her on, especially after listening to those wolves. She moaned softly.

"I'm going to take that as a yes." He reached for the front button of her slacks. "But stop me if that isn't what you meant."

"Zach, you really should…" She didn't finish the weak protest because he'd slipped his hand inside her panties and discovered for himself that her answer was yes to whatever he had in mind.

His husky murmur of appreciation aroused her even more. His voice rasped in the stillness. "Kick off your shoes."

She understood why. He had no intention of taking her back to his tiny bedroom. He wanted her to strip right here, in the open doorway.

Apparently lust trumped modesty and her fear of wild animals, because she was going to let him do that. Once she was naked from the waist down, she wasn't surprised when he turned her toward a counter beside the door and asked her to brace her hands on it.

Her pulse beat frantically as she imagined having sex in a doorway open to the night air. No one could see or hear them, no one but the creatures of the forest. That seemed even more erotic. She had her own wild animal here in the trailer with her, and acting out his fantasy excited her more than he knew.

The condom box just happened to be in one of the shopping bags at her feet, and he wasted no time finding it. Cool air touched her bare bottom and the hot, moist place where he would soon bury his cock. She shivered, this time in anticipation instead of fear.

"Mmm, Jeannette." His breathing was ragged as he grasped her hips. "You drive me crazy." He probed once and sucked in a breath. "You're so wet." In one swift movement, he filled her, his groan thick with desire.

She gasped with pleasure as his cock twitched and his thighs brushed hers.

Supporting her and helping her balance, he eased back and slid home again. This time his groan was louder. "It feels too good." His voice was tight with strain. "I want it too much."

Her chest heaved as she struggled for air. "Go... for it."

"I...I have to." He began to stroke slowly at first, but that pace didn't last long. Soon he was pumping wildly as his thighs slapped hers. His noisy gusts of breath turned into stifled sounds punctuated with hoarse swearwords.

His frenzy fueled hers and she hurtled toward her climax. When their movements had reached a fever pitch, he slipped one hand forward to cup her, holding her for his thrusts as he massaged her trigger point.

She came before he did, panting and whimpering as her release surged through her. Her knees might have given way if he hadn't gripped her tight, one hand at her hip and one between her legs. Then he drove home one last time with a bellow of triumph. His body shuddered against hers and he swore once more as he pulsed within her.

They stayed like that for several long seconds until their breathing no longer sounded like the tortured gasps of two long-distance runners.

Zach spoke first. "Wow."

"Yeah."

"Intense."

"Uh-huh."

"If I let go, will you fall down?"

She took inventory. Her legs felt rubbery but she had a tight grip on the counter. "No."

"I'll go slow."

"Please do." She felt a sense of loss as he withdrew. Now that they weren't making so much noise, she heard a cricket tuning up outside. The owl hooted again. Some creature moved through the bushes.

But she experienced the sounds differently now. Pushing herself upright, she turned toward the open door and unbuttoned her blouse. The breeze felt heavenly on her overheated body, so she took off both her blouse and her bra.

Standing naked in front of the open doorway, she no longer felt so alien, so out of place. Sure, she'd freak out if a bear came wandering by. She might be ready to embrace nature, but she also would continue to have a healthy respect for it.

"If you'd let me, I'd take a picture of you like that."

She didn't turn around. "Well, I won't let you."

"Then I'll take a mental picture." Once again he came up behind her and gathered her close. "I've never seen anything so beautiful as you standing naked in the open doorway of my trailer."

"Well, I was danged hot, and there's a nice breeze."

"Logical. Is that all there is to it?"

"No." She leaned her head against his shoulder. "Thank you for what just happened."

"Hey, I'm the one full of gratitude. I honestly didn't think you'd agree. You seemed really nervous when we arrived, but I wanted to hear the wolves, and I was hoping you'd be open to the mysterious beauty of the place."

"I *was* nervous at first. But then the wolves started howlin', and you got turned on, which turned me on, and one thing led to another."

He laughed and gave her a hug. "It sure did."

"We behaved a little bit like animals do."

"I know. That's what I wanted."

"And because you wanted that, I began to want it, and now…it's as if some switch was tripped when we had sex that way, with the door open to the night. I feel as if I'm just another animal out here in the forest. It's kind of nice. Liberating."

He sighed. "That's great. I can't tell you how happy that makes me."

"That doesn't mean I'm ready to get up close and personal with a bear, though. I'm still scared of them."

"That's okay. I'd rather you didn't decide to get chummy with a bear. But like I said, I haven't seen one yet, and I've camped here for a month. For you to catch a glimpse of one in the next two days would be astounding."

"I don't know, Zach. Astounding things keep happening to me. But I could pass on seeing a bear." Now that she was braver, though, she wouldn't mind seeing one from a great distance.

"It's getting lighter out there. Can you tell? Before the outline of the Tetons wasn't clear, but now it is."

"That means you need to leave in a little while."

"Yeah. I was on probation for my first two weeks until they decided whether or not I could cut it around here. Now that I've been put on permanently, I don't want to screw that up by coming in late."

"Then show me around, tell me anything I need to know about this trailer and take off, cowboy."

"Okay." He gave her a quick hug and released her. "We can start by closing this door. No one will come out here at night, but during the day, it's possible somebody could show up. After all, this is Chance land." He pulled the door closed and twisted the dead bolt. "I'll lock you in when I leave."

"Are you worried about someone coming in?"

"Not a person. The crime rate's really low in the Shoshone area. But raccoons can be tricky. They use those little hands of theirs like you wouldn't believe. If I don't lock the door, they might figure out how to open it."

"I'll remember that."

"They're mostly nocturnal, so it's not a huge risk during the day, but I'm in the habit of locking the door just in case."

"Understood."

"Hang on a minute. I'm going to get you something." He walked back toward what she'd identified as the bedroom.

"If it's a weapon of some kind, I don't want it." She took in the extensive wood paneling covering many of the surfaces. Although the shape of the Airstream was nothing like a boat, she was reminded of sailing on her parents' yacht.

"It's not a weapon." He ducked through the bedroom doorway, although the door was merely a navy curtain secured with a tailored band of material. When he came back, he held out a navy bathrobe. "This is mine, and if you'd put it on, I'd be appreciative."

"All right." The bathrobe engulfed her, but it carried his spicy scent, so she didn't mind its enormous size. At least it didn't drag on the floor. He'd chosen knee-length, which was ankle-length on her. She belted it securely and rolled up the sleeves. "Better?"

He smiled. "I'm not sure. You look damned cute in it, so even though you're covered up, I want to do you."

"I could lock myself in the bathroom and we could talk through the door."

"Nah. I'll be strong. The robe does help. Just not enough. I'm not sure anything would, to tell the truth. I have a serious case of lust for you, Jeannette Trenton."

"That cuts both ways, Zach Powell."

"That's something. At least we're in the same fix." His gaze was warm and he seemed to lose his place in the conversation.

Through the window, she could see the sky was turning the color of his gray eyes. "You were going to acquaint me with the silver bullet," she prompted.

"Yes. Yes, I was." He gestured toward the end opposite his bedroom. "That's the sitting area. A tabletop folds down and it becomes the dining room." Once again, he became lost staring at her.

"Lord, boy, you need sleep. You keep spacin' out

on me." She should feel guilty that she'd been part of the scenario that had kept him from sleeping, but she knew he wouldn't have given that up for anything.

He shook his head as if to clear it. "I'll be fine. Where was I?"

"The couch is there, and a table folds down so you can eat there, too. I already know the bedroom's at the other end, and I can see the kitchen's in the middle. I assume the bathroom is, too."

"Right. There's food in the refrigerator. If you get hungry, help yourself."

"What about you? I completely forgot about your breakfast!"

"I'll grab something during a break at the ranch. The hands keep snacks in the bunkhouse. They're great guys and they've told me I'm welcome to it."

"You really love it here, don't you?"

"I do."

"And you don't miss the intellectual challenge of your legal practice?"

"Not at all."

She caught the flicker in his gray eyes. He might be telling himself he didn't miss it, but he'd been to- tally involved in the case she'd presented to him dur- ing the drive to Jackson. Now wasn't the time to argue that point, though.

"I expect you to sleep most of the time I'm gone, though."

She laughed. "Are you ordering me to bed?"

"I wish I could, and then follow you in there. In fact, if you wouldn't mind tucking yourself in right now while I'm being noble and strong, I won't be tempted to kiss you goodbye."

She met his gaze. He yearned for more time together and so did she. After what they'd shared, a
kiss goodbye would be a natural thing to do, but one
kiss would turn into twenty, and he'd be late to work.

"I'll see you later, Zach."

"See you later, Jeannette."

She turned and walked back toward the curtained
doorway. It was a little goodbye, not the big one that
would come in a couple of days. If she had trouble
parting from him now, what would Monday be like?

9

Zach put in a couple of hours doing the usual morning chores, feeding horses and mucking out stalls. That kind of manual labor allowed him to think. The more he considered the step that he and Jeannette had taken by sharing living quarters this weekend, the more he realized he needed to inform Jack ASAP.

Jeannette had left a note at the Bunk and Grub, so word might eventually filter to the ranch. But Pam was spending the night in Emmett's little house and might have decided to stay until after the party. The grapevine wouldn't be working as efficiently as it might otherwise.

Zach felt an obligation both to Jeannette and the Chance family to make sure the new arrangement didn't catch everyone by surprise, especially in the middle of what was supposed to be Regan and Lily's show. Jeannette had mentioned that she didn't want to mess up their party by creating gossip. As the head of the family, Jack should be notified, and soon.

Fortunately Jack was on the premises this morning. The Last Chance was throwing a party tonight, and as the host, Jack was supervising every aspect of it. According to the old-timers, he'd gone through a period when he didn't want to have anything to do with parties or the planning of them.

But marriage and fatherhood had changed him and now he wanted to know every last detail, to the point that some complained that he'd overcorrected. As for Zach, he was thrilled the guy was on hand today so they could discuss Jeannette.

He found the eldest Chance brother helping the ranch hands set up a platform that would serve as a bandstand and dance floor. Judging from the conversation, the platform had been erected and dismantled several times in the past few years. It looked a little the worse for wear.

"It'll be fine for one more event." A hammer held loosely in one hand, Jack was talking with Watkins, a stocky ranch hand with a carefully waxed handlebar mustache. Watkins would be playing guitar for the event, along with a younger hand named Trey.

"I'm not convinced," Watkins said. "Trey and me, we invested in new speakers and they're heavier than the ones we used to have. Plus once people start dancing, if they stomp around like usual, they'll stress those joints."

"It's gonna work," Jack said. "After this party, we'll turn it into firewood and start over, but this is the last event of the season and I hate like hell to invest in a new platform that will just sit all winter in the tractor barn. And we're running out of time." He caught sight of Zach standing nearby. "What do you think, Powell?"

He shrugged. "I'm no expert."

Jack walked over to him and lowered his voice. "You've eyeballed contracts for rock concerts. You must have an opinion about the logistics, even for something piddly like this deal. Give me what you got, man."

After assessing the platform and thinking about the potential dangers, Zach shrugged. "Like I said, this isn't my area, but I've seen what can happen when things go wrong. In your shoes, I wouldn't risk it. I'd call in all the hands if you have to so you can build a new platform."

"You're right. I know you're right. I've just been trying to convince myself by trying to convince Watkins." He adjusted the fit of his black Stetson before calling out to the hands. "We're starting over! Watkins, head into town and rustle us up some wood."

The stocky cowboy grinned. "Good decision, boss."

"It's an expensive decision, and we'll need everybody's help." He turned to another cowhand. "Shorty, put out the word. We need a new platform by five." Then he turned to Zach. "How are you with a hammer and saw?"

"Not bad. I'll help. But that wasn't why I came looking for you."

Jack's gaze narrowed. "I hope you're not giving me your notice. I realize you're overeducated for this job, but I like you and I'm hoping you stick it out."

"I plan to stick it out. This isn't about me. It's about Jeannette Trenton."

Jack's expression became unreadable. "What about her?"

"She's staying in my Airstream for the weekend."

"She's *what?*"

"I invited her and she accepted. Do you have a problem with that?"

"I don't know yet. The words are still making their way from my ears to my brain. Wasn't she at the Bunk and Grub or did I make that up?"

"She was at the Bunk and Grub, but she…I mean *we* decided she'd enjoy…uh, that is, we thought—"

"Easy, cowboy. Don't strain your brain." Jack tipped his hat back and scrubbed a hand over his face. "I'm putting it all together, now. Josie told me that you and Jeannette were heading off to Jackson so she could buy more appropriate clothes for this weekend. I guess that shopping trip went well, huh?"

"She's a lawyer. I'm a lawyer. We have a lot in common."

"I can see that."

"Anyway, I just wanted you to know."

Jack nodded. "Thanks."

"And she'll be coming to the party with me."

"I figured as much. Is she still leaving town on Monday?"

"Far as I know." His chest tightened at the thought.

"You just said you plan to stick it out here, so I'll take that to mean you won't be running off to Virginia anytime soon."

"Definitely not."

Jack tapped the hammer handle against his thigh. "Okay, then." He turned toward the platform. "Might as well start turning this into kindling. We'll be needing it come December. Ever wintered in snow country?"

"Nope."

"When six-foot drifts block the front door and the wind chill is forty below, a man finds out what he's made of."

"Good." Zach grinned at him. "I'm looking forward to it."

ZACH'S DOUBLE BED tucked under the paneled curve of the Airstream's roof combined with the closed blinds over the windows gave the nook a cavelike quality that made her think of hibernating bears. His soft sheets and light blanket carried the scent of his aftershave. Although she was exhausted, she couldn't go to sleep right away. She kept thinking of Zach and all they'd shared.

Eventually she did fall asleep, though, and when she woke up she spent a couple of seconds trying to figure out where she was. Her nose registered the answer first. She was in Zach's bed, in Zach's silver bullet of a trailer, in a wooded area of the Last Chance Ranch.

The bedroom was tiny and didn't have space for much more than the bed, but a small ledge on the door wall held a clock. Nearly one in the afternoon. Zach got off work at two. Picturing him coming through the front door in another hour or so sent a jolt of anticipation through her.

Meeting him had changed everything, and seemed to be changing her, too. She never would have guessed she'd agree to make love in front of a door open to the wilds of Wyoming. Remembering it made her laugh in delight. She could take a solar shower with him this afternoon, no problem.

His solid presence gave her courage in so many

ways. Until he'd come on the scene, she'd dreaded
Regan and Lily's engagement party even though at-
tending seemed like the right thing to do. She was
still such an outsider that she'd expected to struggle
through the evening. Having Zach by her side would
make all the difference.

Thinking of the coolness that had surrounded them
when they'd made love in the wee morning hours
made her aware that the air was close and warm. Getting to her knees on the bed, she pulled up the blinds
on all three windows that wrapped around the front
of the trailer. Then she cranked each one open.

Ah. A breeze filled the bedroom with the aroma
of evergreens. Birds chirped in the trees, and the bur-
ble of the stream created a scene right out of a nature
video. She could see why Zach loved it here, but the
weather wouldn't always be this gorgeous.

She'd researched Jackson Hole after becoming engaged to Regan because he'd talked about taking her
to the ranch. Summers had sounded great and this visit
had convinced her how wonderful they could be. But
winters were seriously frigid and snowy in this area.
She wondered how Zach planned to deal with snow,
ice and subzero weather.

Maybe he hadn't thought of that, yet. He seemed
to be living his new life day-by-day, which interested
her. She'd always been a planner, but he didn't seem
to have definite plans for the future.

Her stomach rumbled. Zach would probably eat
lunch at the ranch, so since she was hungry, she should
feed herself before he came back. Besides, she was curious about the trailer. Now that she was more rested,

she wanted to explore it, although that exploration wouldn't take long.

Grabbing Zach's bathrobe from where she'd left it at the end of the bed, she put it on. He had said that people sometimes showed up here during daylight hours. She didn't want to be seen wandering around his trailer stark naked.

She expected to find her clothes scattered on the floor where she'd shed them, but apparently Zach had gathered them before leaving. They lay folded on her suitcase, which stood right where he'd left it when they first came in. Both shopping bags sat beside the suitcase.

She knew for a fact Zach was glad she'd moved in for the weekend, but she didn't want him tripping over her things. With the limited space in the trailer, she wasn't sure what she would do with the suitcase, the bags or her clothes. She'd figure something out after lunch.

The blinds had been pulled up in the kitchen and living/dining area, so she opened those windows, too. Sunlight filtered through the trees, creating a dappled pattern on the walls, floor and built-in furniture. She noticed a rainbow dancing along one wall and traced it to a sun catcher Zach had hung from the ceiling near one of the windows. It shivered in the breeze.

A small plaque on another wall depicted a rustic log cabin and the words *Happiness is a cabin in the woods*. She wondered if he hoped to buy or build a cabin eventually somewhere in the area. That would answer the question of how he'd get through the winters, and it also told her he'd found his bliss in Jackson Hole.

Out of habit, she picked up her purse from the counter and pulled out her phone. To her surprise, there was a text from Zach. Now she remembered that they'd exchanged numbers on the way home from Jackson, in between belting out rock tunes.

Apparently he'd been asked to stay later to help build a new dance platform for the party tonight. He'd be back in time to shower and change. She hoped he was holding up okay without sleep. A nap would have helped, although knowing him, he might not have agreed to sleep when they could make love instead.

No text from Erin, though, so the research on the case must be going better thanks to Zach's suggestions. The law office seemed a million miles away as she tucked her phone back in her purse. In two short steps she stood in front of the cupboards and the refrigerator. Compact living took some getting used to.

She hoped to find food items that wouldn't take major cooking skills. She'd already screwed up a kitchen experience once on this trip and she didn't relish doing it again here. This place belonged to a guy, so she thought her chances were good that simple food would be available.

The kitchen yielded a jar of peanut butter, smooth, the way she liked it, apricot jam, also a favorite of hers, and a loaf of bread. His coffeepot was simple enough to operate, and before long she'd pulled down the collapsible dining table and was eating her first meal in his silver bullet.

This setting was seductive, making her want to walk in the woods after lunch and read a book while sitting next to the stream. Unlike Zach, she still needed to earn a living, but she'd saved some money, too. If she scaled back her lifestyle, she could take a part-time job and still make ends meet.

If she stayed here long enough, would she lose all ambition the way Zach seemed to have done? She didn't want to find out. She'd worked too long and hard to achieve her success, and a partnership was something she'd envisioned from the beginning. It was within reach. She wanted that validation.

But thinking of reading beside the stream reminded her that a book would be nice to have while she ate. Leaving the table, she walked three steps to his bookshelf. Maybe the Airstream reminded her of a boat partly because everything had to be secured against falling in transit. Railings kept both food and cookware in the cupboards, and reading material from falling off the bookshelf.

She browsed his selection of action/adventure novels and decided against those. He had a few mysteries that interested her. He also had trail guides and a selection of outdoor living magazines. His manual for the Airstream was tucked in with the magazines, which made her smile.

Behind the magazines she discovered something surprising, though. In spite of his firm statement that he had no interest in practicing law, he'd bought a study guide for passing the Wyoming bar exam. It looked and smelled brand-new. She paged through it, hoping to find some jotted notes or a dog-eared page, anything to indicate he'd spent time with the material. Nothing.

Yet he'd bought it. She clung to that thought as evidence that he might yet resume the profession he'd trained for. Replacing the study guide exactly as she'd found it, she took a paperback mystery from the shelf and returned to the table.

The book stayed closed as she wrestled with her thoughts. It shouldn't matter to her whether Zach abandoned his career. He obviously intended to stay in this area, and whether he worked as a lawyer or a ranch hand wouldn't affect her one bit.

But that wasn't the whole story, and she knew it. She believed that everyone came into this world with certain gifts, and using them fully contributed to a satisfying life. That's what she wanted for herself and for anyone sharing her journey.

In discussing her Thoroughbred-foal case with him, she'd discovered that he had a mind perfectly suited to the intricacies of contract law. She knew that because she had the same gift. Physically they were a great match, but they were also in tune mentally. No wonder they'd bonded so fast.

Sure, circumstances might keep them apart, namely his decision to live here and her career opportunities in Virginia. But that problem wasn't the biggest sticking point between them. She purely hated that he was wasting his potential.

She'd agreed to this sexual adventure because she'd desperately needed a night of fantasy and Zach had been eager to share that with her. Now the adventure would last longer than one night, but the boundaries hadn't really changed. She was still leaving on Monday.

They could continue having great sex until she left and keep those boundaries in place. Until finding that study guide, she'd expected to do exactly that. She hadn't intended to involve herself in his future.

But now she planned to open up this can of worms. If he loved working on the ranch, great. Surely he could satisfy that urge and still use his top-notch legal mind in some capacity. If he chose not to, well, that was his right, of course.

If she were more Zen maybe she'd be able to accept it. She wasn't Zen. Before she left on Monday, they were going to talk about that study guide. Maybe the discussion would blow up in her face, but she had to give it a shot.

As she finished her PB and J and sipped her coffee, she decided to choose that moment very carefully. So much could depend on how such a discussion ended. She certainly wouldn't hit him with it when he walked in the door this afternoon.

Between now and then she had some tidying up to do. Rolling back the sleeves of his bathrobe a couple more turns, she washed up her lunch dishes. Then she tackled the suitcase and shopping-bag situation.

Miracle of miracles, she found two empty drawers in the hallway. She transferred the contents of her suitcase and the bags to the large drawers. She put the box of condoms on the ledge in the bedroom next to the clock.

She'd brought a pair of flip-flops, and she put those on while she carried her empty suitcase to the car.

Zach pulled up just as she opened the back door of her rental car to hoist the suitcase inside. He hopped out and rounded the front of his truck. "I hope this isn't what it looks like." His tone was joking, but there was a slight frown denting the space between his eyebrows.

"The suitcase is empty."

"That's good news." The frown disappeared and he nudged back his hat. "For a minute there I wondered if you were moving out."

"Nope." She closed the door and walked over to him. "Just tryin' to keep the floor clear of obstacles."

He smiled. "Good thinking." Hooking his finger in the bathrobe's tie, he tugged her closer and loosened the tie in the process. "Missed you."

"I missed you, too." She'd noticed sawdust on his jeans, which matched the heady aroma of freshly cut lumber and manly sweat. Her body responded with astounding speed. "You're early."

"We finished up sooner than expected." He slid both hands inside the bathrobe, loosening the tie completely as he drew her into his arms. "So I hotfooted it home only to find you slinging your suitcase into your car. I immediately started coming up with what I could say or do to keep you from taking off."

She wound her arms around his neck and nestled against him. The cool metal of his belt buckle pressed against her warm skin. "Like what?"

"Like telling you how much fun you're going to have under my solar shower." He massaged her bottom.

"I will?"

"Guaranteed. If you haven't been soaped, sponged and rinsed off by Zach Powell, you have no idea what you're missing."

"Can't wait."

"I'm afraid you'll have to." He lowered his head and gave her a kiss that included a very erotic use of his tongue. Finally he lifted his mouth a fraction from hers. "The thing is," he murmured, "because I'm back early, we have some time to kill before we shower. And I have some ideas about that, too."

"I'll just bet you do."

"How do you like my bed?"

"Love it."

"I predict you'll love it even more with a couple of enhancements."

"Which are?"

"Me and a condom."

10

ZACH RELISHED EVERY HOT, heavy-breathing moment with Jeannette in his double bed, even if they were a little cramped and he bumped his head. Twice. That was the number of times she'd come, and he was so involved in her enthusiastic response that he forgot the space constraints.

He came soon after her second orgasm, which canceled out the pain in his head right quick. Eventually he had to exit the bedroom and go into the airplane-sized bathroom to dispose of the condom. Knowing the solar shower was next on the agenda, he grabbed a couple of towels on his way back.

He walked in to find her lying there all pink and mussed from their great sex. She rolled to her side and smiled at him. He realized then that he was well and truly screwed, and not in the way he would have preferred.

Weeks, months, maybe years would go by before he could sleep in that bed without being reminded of Jeannette. The hot sex was part of it, but he loved the way she looked lying there, especially at this very moment, her green eyes smoky and her body relaxed and languid.

Despite knowing the memories would haunt him, he would give anything not to have this party obligation. Although every intimate second he spent with her dug the hole deeper, he longed to hide away with this woman. They wouldn't have to make love constantly. He was willing to take time out to eat and talk. In fact, talking to her was one of the best parts.

In short, he was falling in love. And that was why he was screwed six ways to Sunday. He wasn't right for her and she wasn't right for him. They'd both known it in advance, and like a fool, he'd thought he could handle this temporary arrangement.

Well, he'd just have to, wouldn't he? Not much choice in the matter. He wasn't going to ask her to give up all she'd worked for in Virginia to start over in Jackson Hole so she could hang out with him. He knew what it took to build a practice from scratch. She'd be justified in laughing at the idea.

Maybe the party was a good thing. It would get them out of here for a few hours so he could pull back emotionally. He adopted the drill-sergeant voice he'd learned from watching movies. "Time to hit the showers, Trenton!"

"Aye, aye, sir." She gave him a sloppy salute and stayed where she was.

"I said move it!"

"Somebody turned my bones to rubber, sir."

"Tell me who that son of a bitch was and I'll have him thrown in the brig!"

"Only if you'll throw me in there, too, sir. I want him to do it again."

His cock stirred. "Trust me, he wants to." His voice grew husky. "But he promised to take you to a party."

"I know." She sighed. "And the party's important. I need to get into that shower."

"It'll be a very good shower." He waggled his eyebrows.

"I see." She sat up and swung her feet to the floor. "You're turning me into a libertine, Zach Powell. All I can think of is having sex with you in all sorts of imaginative ways."

"I'll take that as a compliment."

"You should. You're looking at a type-A personality who always puts business before pleasure."

"It takes one to know one."

She shook her head. "If you were that way once, you're not now."

"You'd be surprised. I could revert in no time." That was one of the reasons he wouldn't go back to practicing law. He was a recovering type-A personality, if there were such a thing.

"Does it make you nervous to be around someone like me, then?"

"A little bit." He grinned. "But then I can get you naked and make you come, and we're all good."

"So that's your method." She stood and walked toward him. "FYI, it works like a charm."

"For now, anyway." He didn't kid himself. He knew when she was back in lawyer mode that his strategy would be less effective. He'd caught her at a time when she needed the distraction he was willing to provide. "Ready for the solar-shower experience?"

"Why not? What should I bring?"

"Just your sweet body. You can put on your flip-flops if you want. I'm used to walking barefoot on the ground, but you're not. The soap and sponges are already out there."

"We're leaving the trailer wearing nothing? I thought you said it was always possible someone would come by."

"Normally that's true, but everyone and his dog is working furiously to get ready for the party. They're either setting up tables and chairs, fixing food or getting dressed. No one has time to take a trip out to check on you and me."

"What about some stranger?"

"We're on private property. A stranger would be trespassing, and Jack doesn't tolerate trespassers. He takes his stewardship of this land very seriously. Not much happens on the Last Chance that escapes his notice."

"Including me staying out here with you?"

"I told him about that this morning."

She looked wary. "What did he say?"

"Not much. He was surprised at first, but in the long run, I think he figures it's our business." He thought about whether to add any more, and decided she might be reassured if he mentioned what else had been said. "He wanted to make sure I wouldn't be heading for Virginia in the near future. I said there was no chance of that."

"Of course not. I can tell how much you love it here."

"Anyway, Jack understands this deal between us is temporary."

"That's good."

"I thought so. I didn't want any speculation on anyone's part. Jack will probably inform Josie, and the word will get out."

"At least I know Regan will be fine with it."

Zach started to say that he couldn't care less. He'd been the one to offer Jeannette support when Regan had been otherwise occupied, so the guy was in no position to say anything about the situation now. But he thought better of saying so. "But if we don't take showers, we'll never get there, which would not be a good thing."

"Right. Lead the way."

He grabbed his keys on the way out the door and locked up after them to make sure nothing got in while they were engrossed in the shower. He'd checked the time and they had some leeway. They could have some fun with the shower.

The relaxation they'd both felt after rolling around on his bed had disappeared during their discussion. The shower would be another tension reliever. Nothing like warm water, a smooth bar of soap and a soft sponge to make them both feel great.

He was proud of this shower setup. The Airstream had one, but he was always knocking his knees and elbows against the wall in there. His solar shower gave him all the room he needed, and it didn't use any energy other than sunlight.

He'd built a wooden drainage platform and positioned it under the bag of water hanging from a tree branch, and the trench he'd dug carried water away so he didn't end up with a mud hole. A bamboo shower caddy hanging from the trunk of the tree held his soap, shampoo and a sponge.

Jeannette surveyed his creation. "This is amazing, Zach. Everyone should have something like this."

"That would be great except not everyone has acres of private land surrounding them, and come winter, I won't be using this anymore."

"I've wondered what will happen with you and this trailer after the first snow."

"I'm working on that. I have some ideas. I've only been here a month."

"I know. And for the summer, you're in great shape. So what happens first with this shower situation?"

"Do you want to wash your hair? I recommend it because I don't have a shower cap."

She peered at his shampoo. "Okay, sure. Not my brand, but it'll do."

The scene seemed somewhat unreal. He'd been out here nearly every afternoon for a month and had begun taking the routine for granted. Seeing Jeannette standing there in all her glory put a whole new erotic spin on things. He had a little trouble concentrating on the task at hand.

She peered at him. "So what next?"

"I have to get you wet."

Her green eyes sparkled. "That's usually no problem."

Lust hardened his cock. "Uh, with water."

"Oh, *that's* what you're talking about. You'll have to be more specific."

He cleared his throat. "I'll try to remember that. First thing, get up on the platform."

"With or without flip-flops?"

"Without. I sanded the wood until it was like satin. You'll like standing on it."

"Gotcha." She stepped out of her rubber sandals and onto the platform. "You're right. This feels great under my toes. Now what?"

"I'll release some water from the bag. Get under it and use your hands to work it through your hair and spread it over your body."

"Sounds kinky."

"It's not when I do it."

"You don't have a little solo fun in this shower?"

"No. I'm outside, for God's sake. I'm not going to…"

"Then we won't be fooling around out here?"

He realized all the plans he had for her. They would still be outside, and he'd specifically imagined using the sponge to make her a happy woman. "I didn't say that."

"But you don't fool around alone."

"That's different."

"Why?"

He stared at her as he tried to come up with a reasonable explanation as to why he was perfectly willing to make her come during this shower experience, but he'd never considered taking his own pleasure that way.

"You don't have an answer, do you?"

"No."

"Then here's the deal. You can play around with me all you want, but then you have to let me have the same liberties. Because I'm getting into this outdoor recreation plan. Now that you've convinced me we won't be observed except for the birds and the bees, I'm all for it."

"Then so am I." Hell, why quibble? He had her here

for a very short time, and he might as well get as much enjoyment out of those precious hours as possible.

She gazed up at the spigot. "Now that we've settled that, turn on the water. And don't use too much."

"I won't." He opened the valve.

"I want plenty left for my turn with you."

That comment distracted him so much that he forgot to turn off the water.

"Zach!"

He shut it off again.

"That was too much water. I know it was."

"Maybe."

"I'm guessing I should wash my hair before you move in with whatever you have in mind. Otherwise I'll get soap in my eyes."

He grinned. His seductive operation was being taken over by this newly liberated woman and he was fine with that. "Sure. Get some suds in your hair and then I'll give you more water to wash them out." Then he had a thought. "Or I could wash your hair."

She paused with her hand cupped, shampoo pooled in her palm. "I suppose you could. Do you want to?"

"Silly question." He stepped onto the platform, took her hand and transferred the slippery shampoo to his palm. Standing behind her, his body brushing hers, he began working the lather into her hair. "Are your eyes closed?" He didn't want to get soap in them.

"Yes."

"Well, tip your head back some more to make sure nothing runs into them." He massaged her scalp with the tips of his fingers. "Am I doing it right? I've never washed anyone's hair but mine."

"You're doing…great." Her words tumbled out along with a soft purr of contentment.

"Don't know why I never have. This is fun. Especially naked."

"Mmm."

"Eyes still closed?" He leaned over her shoulder to make sure and discovered her nipples were tight with arousal. He was turning her on by washing her hair. He'd had no clue that would happen.

He hated to rinse her hair and break the mood he had going. Figuring that shampoo wasn't much different from liquid soap, he stroked the lather over her shoulders. Next he covered her breasts with his hands and massaged in slow circles.

She moaned softly and leaned against him, which brought her sleek behind in contact with his increasingly rigid cock. Sweet torture. He reached a hand between her thighs and caressed her with deliberate intent.

Her breathing changed as she rose on her toes and rocked her hips forward, inviting him deeper. Ah, there. Curving his fingers to stroke her G-spot brought a throaty groan of delight.

Her moist channel flexed and he pressed his thumb on her sensitive nub. For one moment she was as taut as a bow, poised on the brink, and then she came, his name on her lips as her body surrendered to the surge of her orgasm.

He held her until she stopped shaking. Continuing to support her with one hand, he reached for the valve that sent a spray of warm water onto them. "Keep your eyes shut," he murmured as he worked the suds from her hair. He followed the trail of lather down her body, wiping it away with his wet hands.

He let the water run to make sure the shampoo was all gone. He wouldn't have enough for his shower, but he didn't care. When he was convinced she was rinsed clean, he reached for the valve, but she chose that moment to turn in his arms and wrap her fingers around his cock.

Droplets clung to her eyelashes as she gazed up at him. Her mouth curved seductively. "My turn." She began to slide her fingers rapidly up and down as warm water sluiced over them, aiding her cause.

There couldn't be much water left and this was a far better use of it than any shower would ever be. He'd been aroused ever since he'd started washing her hair. He would come quickly. She held his gaze as she stroked, and his climax arrived right before the water ran out. Shuddering, he pulled her slick body close.

He had no wish to let her go, but they couldn't stand out here forever. With great reluctance he sighed and released her. He'd lost track of the time, but judging from the lengthening shadows, they needed to move along.

She gave him a lazy smile. "I liked that."

"Me, too."

She noticed the empty water bag. "It's all gone and you didn't get your shower."

"I'll take one inside." His voice was husky, his body still humming. If they didn't have to leave he'd invite her back to bed. But they had places to go and people to see.

"I love your solar shower."

He reached out and combed a damp strand of hair back from her cheek. "I knew you would."

"Tomorrow, you get to be first. And I'll wash *your* hair. I promise it will turn you on like you wouldn't believe."

He chuckled. "Yeah, like my libido needs a boost. I've never had so much sex in my life. Never wanted to. But with you, I can't seem to get enough. You're amazing."

Her expression grew serious. "It's not me. It's the tickin' clock."

He didn't want to believe that, but he didn't feel like arguing about it, either. "Oh, I'm pretty sure it's you. Clocks do nothing for me whatsoever."

"You know what I mean." She smiled. "We—"

"Shh." He laid a finger over her mouth. "I do know, and I think you're wrong, but let's debate it later, preferably in bed after we're sweaty and satisfied. Right now, we're expected at an engagement party. You don't want to miss it."

"Guess not."

"If you don't go to the party, you can't show off the clothes you bought in Jackson." He picked up her flip-flops and knelt down to slip them on her feet.

"When you do that, you make me feel like Cinderella."

He stood and held out his hand. "And you make me feel like Prince Charming. Will you dance with me at the ball, princess?"

"Do you dance?" She seemed intrigued with the idea.

"Jack expects all his cowhands to know how. He claims it's an important part of the cowboy way and should be encouraged whenever possible. Fortunately I had that covered before I hired on." He gazed at her. "Do *you* dance?"

"I'm a Southern belle. I had a comin'-out party. Of course I dance."

"Then we're good. But let's not stay until the clock strikes twelve, okay?"

"Will you turn into a pumpkin?"

"No. I'll turn into a frustrated cowboy with an erection. I'm in danger of that right now, in fact. Let's get you back to the trailer and into those new clothes."

She laughed. "Okay."

As they walked over to the trailer hand-in-hand, he wished they hadn't done a riff on that particular fairy tale. It was all about a ticking clock.

11

Zach didn't have full-length mirrors in his trailer, but he convinced her she looked like a cowgirl in her new outfit of jeans and a white stretchy knit top that showed off a little cleavage. "A sexy cowgirl, at that," he said with a smile.

"Thank you." She watched him finish getting dressed in the living room. It was the only place big enough to accomplish the task, so she'd dressed while he'd showered in the minuscule bathroom. "But I don't want to seem as if I'm tryin' too hard. My mama used to caution me about it. I have that tendency."

His jaw tightened. "We all try too hard sometimes." He fastened the last few snaps on his dove-grey Western shirt. "I'm not sure it helps to point it out."

She thought about that. "I suppose not. I guess she meant well, but I used to get a knot in my stomach when she said I was tryin' too hard."

"How's your stomach feeling now?" He unfastened his jeans and tucked his shirttails inside.

"Warm and happy. All of me is warm and happy

watchin' you get dressed. The only thing that would be better is watching you get undressed."

He sighed as he buckled his belt. "Don't I wish you could be doing that right now." He opened a cupboard and pulled out what looked like a new black Stetson and put it on. "Ready?"

"Sure." Oh, yeah, she was, but not to be with a bunch of other people. She wanted to have this broad-shouldered, sweet-smelling man all to herself. "Nice hat."

"It's my party hat. The gray one's for going into town, and the brown one's for getting dusty working on the ranch. This one's special."

"That's a reason for me to be excited about going tonight, then. You look mighty fine, cowboy."

He touched the brim of his hat. "Thank you, ma'am."

"Did you practice that?"

He grinned. "I might have a time or two, after I bought my first hat."

"Well, it's extremely effective. It made my little heart flutter."

"Interesting. Did it have any effect on the rest of you?"

She ran a finger down his chest and batted her eyelashes. "*May*-be. Wanna find out?"

"Yes, damn it." With a growl, he set his hands on her shoulders and turned her toward the door. "Get on out of here before I forget all my good intentions."

Laughing, she opened the trailer door and walked down the steps.

He locked up the Airstream but still managed to get the door of his truck open before she reached it.

"I do love the fit of those jeans, lady. And the little sparkles on the back pockets make me think of things I shouldn't, at least for now. Have you ever line danced?"

"No, why?"

"Because if you decide to try it tonight, you'll drive the guys crazy when you wiggle those rhinestones." He winked and closed the door.

After he rounded the truck and climbed behind the wheel, she glanced at him. "You're good for my ego."

"You're good for mine." He closed the door and buckled up. "I feel like the luckiest guy on the planet tonight." He started the powerful engine and backed the truck around.

"Oh, Lord, I just thought of something."

He stepped on the brakes. "What?"

"I didn't get Lily and Regan anything. I probably should have. It's an engagement party, so I should be bringing them an engagement present. I should have thought of that while we were in Jackson, but I didn't. I was too focused on—"

"Jeannette, it's okay." He put a hand on her thigh and gave it a squeeze. "Just tell them you wanted to ask what they needed and you'll send them a gift from Virginia."

"I know, but I don't even have a card! If I had a card, I could write something like that in it, but I didn't even get that far in my thinking. Sheesh."

Zach put the truck in Reverse. "Let's go see what I have. I'm thinking that I bought a box of note cards a while ago, a mixture for various occasions. I don't write to people much, but every now and then I get the urge."

Somehow, she doubted that he'd happen to have a note card that said Congratulations on Your Engagement. But he was being sweet and understanding, so she'd go back in the trailer with him and see what he had available.

Once they were back in the Airstream, he pulled open a drawer. "Yeah, here's the box." He opened it. "There's one left, but it won't work."

"Why not?"

Laughing, he handed her the card.

The message on the front read In Deepest Sympathy. "I see what you mean." She grinned. "But don't give up. We could tear off the front if the message inside is ambiguous." She opened the card. "'May your memories comfort you in your hour of grief.'" She looked at Zach and they both started laughing like crazy people.

"Oh, yeah." He gasped for breath. "Use the inside part. That's *so* much better!"

"I can think of some couples this card would be great for." She wiped tears from her eyes.

"But not this one. Sorry I haven't solved your problem."

"Yes, you have." She smiled at him. "You made me laugh about it and gave me some perspective. So I don't have a gift and I don't have a card. But I'm here to give them a hug and wish them well in person, so what's the point in a card? And I'm the gift!"

"Yes, you are." He gazed at her with a soft light in his eyes. "You're one hell of a gift. Let's go to that party."

THEY'D BEEN RUNNING behind to begin with, and the issue with the card made them later yet, but Zach watched in admiration as Jeannette shrugged off any trace of discomfort. She stepped right into the party atmosphere with her head high and a bright smile on her face. He stood back while she had a private moment with the honored guests.

Regan and Lily made a striking couple, with his Italian background and her fiery red hair that never seemed quite tidy. Jeannette greeted Regan with a hug. Zach squelched his automatic twinge of jealousy. She'd been Regan's lover once, but now Zach was the fortunate man who shared a bed with her this weekend.

She was blossoming right before his eyes. Although he was happy for her, he struggled with the knowledge that she'd go on blossoming after she left him. Someone else would be around for that and yet he'd helped influence this massive change. That didn't seem fair.

But if he cared about her, and he definitely did, then he should forget about what was fair for him and concentrate on what was right for her. Then he could send her back to Virginia with a glad heart. He wasn't convinced he was that noble, though.

Regan laughed at whatever Jeannette was saying, and Zach felt another twinge. Envy gripped him instead of jealousy as he thought of all the years Regan had known Jeannette and all the memories they shared. She'd probably reminded him of some funny incident just now.

Then Jeannette hugged Lily. After more laughter, the two women started chatting. Zach caught a few words of it and realized they were talking about wedding dresses and veils. Regan's eyes glazed over.

That was Zach's cue to step up and shake the guy's hand. "I'm happy for you. Lily seems like a wonderful woman."

"She has to be if she's willing to put up with the likes of me." Regan turned slightly away from the two women and lowered his voice. "I heard that Jeannette's staying with you for the weekend."

He met Regan's dark gaze. "She is."

"In the Airstream?"

"Yes." Zach braced himself. The guy was the guest of honor, but he'd better watch what he said about Jeannette or things would get ugly fast.

"That's so…" Regan shook his head.

"So what?"

"Out of character."

"Is it?" Zach's hands flexed.

"Take it easy, Powell. I don't mean that as an insult to her or your Airstream. But Jeannette doesn't camp. Or didn't camp." He glanced back in the direction of his bride-to-be and his ex. "Maybe she's changed."

"Could be. I didn't know her before."

"She seems different tonight, more relaxed. The Jeannette I knew would have been mortified to show up without a card or a gift. Instead she made a joke of it."

"Oh?"

"She told us that at the last minute you rummaged around looking for something and came up with a sympathy card."

"That's what you were laughing about?"

"Yeah. I thought it was hilarious, and so did she—

and that surprised the hell out of me. It's good to see her loosening up."

Zach nodded, because he really wasn't sure what to say to that. Fortunately he'd lost the urge to sock Regan in the jaw. Jeannette's ex seemed to genuinely care about her, in spite of what they'd been through.

"Hey, is this a private conversation, or can I join in?" The speaker had a definite Southern drawl.

"Hey, Drake!" Regan gave the newcomer the kind of back-thumping hug that demonstrated affection while asserting manliness. "You know Zach Powell, right? Jack hired him about a month ago."

Drake held out his hand. "Drake Brewster from Virginia. We've never met, but the rumor mills run twenty-four-seven in this town. I saw you with Jeannette a while ago and knew immediately who you were."

Zach accepted the man's firm handshake, thinking this had to be the strangest grouping ever. Here they stood, each of them with an intimate connection to Jeannette. But they couldn't very well mention *that*. He wouldn't, anyway. He searched for some sports-related topic but drew a blank.

Drake had a beer in one hand, but he seemed to be completely sober and every inch the Southern gentleman. The beer didn't seem quite right. It should have been a mint julep, except the Last Chance didn't tend to serve those.

He drew closer to Zach. "This is none of my damn business, but is Jeannette really stayin' in your Airstream for the weekend?"

"Yes." He took a deep breath and hoped Drake would mind his manners, too.

The Southerner glanced over at Regan. "Can you beat that? Our Jeannette camping out?"

Zach would have loved to take issue with the *our Jeannette* part of that comment, but technically Drake and Regan had more right to claim her than he did. They'd both known her since she was eighteen. He'd known her since yesterday.

"It's hard to picture her in a trailer." Regan shrugged. "But I think it's great."

"Oh, so do I. It's just surprisin'." He raised his beer bottle in Zach's direction. "My hat's off to the man who convinced Jeannette Trenton to camp in the woods."

"She's really fine with it." Zach wanted to give credit where credit was due. These guys didn't seem to know anything about Jeannette's spirit of adventure.

Drake's eyes widened. "Seriously?"

"She thought it would be fun." In his opinion, it had shot way past fun and moved into life-changing territory.

"I'll be damned." Drake gazed at Zach with obvious respect. "My hat's still off to you, because somehow you inspired her to consider that option."

"I think she was ready to make some changes. I was just in the right place at the right time."

Drake laughed. "That's soundin' like Lily. Doesn't that sound like her, Regan? 'When the student is ready, the teacher will appear' and all that New Age mumbo jumbo."

"Hey, that's my fiancée you're talking about." But Regan laughed as if he hadn't taken any offence to Drake's comments.

Drake smiled. "I know she is, and I love her to pieces—in a purely platonic way, naturally."

"Naturally."

Zach was fascinated by the dynamic between the two friends. They'd been through hell and back with each other. Drake had seduced Regan's fiancée. And yet they'd rebuilt their trust to the point they could joke about how much Drake loved Lily, but only as a friend.

Zach thought of his conversation with Jeannette on the topic. He still thought it was a tricky juggling act, but maybe a true friendship with a woman who wasn't also a lover might actually be possible. Now that he was out of the hotbed of L.A., he might be able to explore the concept.

A woman called Drake's name and Drake glanced in that direction. "Whoops, gotta go. Tracy's summoning me, and when that woman summons, I respond immediately. Life's easier that way."

Regan laughed. "Wise man." Then he turned to Zach. "What do you say we talk Lily and Jeannette into hitting the buffet table? And I don't know about you, but I could use a beer."

"Sounds good." Zach relaxed. He'd wondered if he'd have to run interference for Jeannette tonight, but Regan's invitation to share dinner had handled that neatly.

Regan might have been preoccupied with his fiancée and wedding plans during the past week, but tonight he seemed keenly aware that Jeannette needed his sponsorship in order to be accepted into this crowd. To Zach's relief, Regan was ready to give it.

During the meal Zach got to know and admire Lily

King, who ran an equine rescue operation on the outskirts of Shoshone. She and Regan had become acquainted when he'd volunteered his vet services there. Zach quickly learned that Lily was way smarter than he was and more generous toward others, too. He put her on his mental list of potential women friends.

And it seemed that once Lily realized Jeannette hadn't truly been accepted by Regan's sisters, she appointed herself the official Jeannette Trenton ambassador. Zach sipped his beer and watched Lily casually bring Jeannette into a group that included two of Regan's sisters, Morgan and Tyler.

Regan followed Zach's gaze. "Lily's working it."

"She sure as hell is. I'm impressed."

"I've tried talking to Morgan and Tyler, but they just brush me off. They want to be affronted on my behalf, and that's that. I was hoping my folks would make it out for this party and they'd talk to my sisters, but at the last minute my mom got the flu so they canceled. Lily will be a big help, though. She's all about peace, love and forgiveness."

"You found yourself a gem, O'Connelli."

"I did. So what about you and Jeannette? Looks like you two get along great."

Zach continued to watch the group of women. Jeannette appeared to be having a good time. "We do get along, but she's about to make partner with her law firm."

"Is she?" Regan grinned. "That's terrific. She didn't tell me that. I'll be sure to congratulate her."

"It is terrific." Zach swallowed another mouthful of beer. "But that means her life is very solid back there. And I've finally found the place I've been looking for.

You live here, so I'm sure you know what I'm talking about. This place gets in your blood."

"It does, which means she could learn to love it, too. Talk her into moving. She's a go-getter. Tell her to set up a law office in Shoshone. We could use one."

Zach considered the very tempting idea. But finally he shook his head. "I can't ask her to give up a partnership she's been working toward for years. She wants it. I think…" He caught himself before he said any more. Probably better not to discuss his theories with Regan.

"Of course she wants it." Regan also continued to watch the group of women talking and laughing. "She's desperate to please her parents."

Zach blew out a breath. "She mentioned something about that."

"I've interacted with Dick and Eunice Trenton over the years, and it's obvious they're more interested in their racing stable than in their daughter. I get the impression she's been tolerated instead of cherished."

"I'm afraid you're right."

"It's a defining part of her story. Because she inconvenienced her parents, she has to be the perfect child. I'm sure they gave her hell over the broken engagement."

Zach nodded. "Sounded like it to me. Unforgiving people with high expectations."

"That's why I was so glad when she blew off the card and present thing. That was a real step forward." Regan turned toward Zach. "If you had anything to do with that, then I have to say you're a good influence on her."

"Maybe I played some small part." He met Regan's

gaze. "But that doesn't mean she'd give up the opportunity to make partner so she could come out here and build a practice from the ground up in a little town like Shoshone. Nothing high-profile about that move. I can't see her doing it."

"Depends on how much she wants to be with you."

Zach took a deep breath. "That's the million-dollar question, isn't it?"

12

JEANNETTE REALIZED WHAT Lily was doing and she thoroughly appreciated it. For the first time since she'd arrived in Shoshone, she had a friendly conversation with Morgan Chance. She made friends with Morgan's two children, both redheads like Morgan, and discussed the real estate business in Shoshone, which was Morgan's field.

She was a little more nervous about talking with Tyler, Regan's twin sister, because she'd heard what a close bond twins could have. Tyler's dark eyes and hair reminded her so much of Regan that she felt as if she knew her and they were already friends. Yet they weren't, and Tyler could be carrying a lot of resentment.

Lily's warm presence helped enormously, though, and soon Tyler opened up. Her former job as an activities director for a cruise line meant she'd traveled the world, including places Jeannette had visited with her parents. Tyler's enthusiasm for beautiful spots like Florence and Santorini melted any remaining tension.

Soon all the women at the table were busy planning their dream vacations.

Unfortunately Cassidy, Regan's eighteen-year-old sister, wasn't sitting with them. She'd made no effort to be friendly and probably wouldn't be easy to win over, but Jeannette was encouraged by the interaction with Morgan and Tyler. Cassidy would just take a little longer. If only Jeannette had more time…but she didn't.

In about thirty-six hours, she'd be on a plane to Virginia. Would she be back? That was hard to say. She loved Regan like a brother and his sisters were a hoot, but popping in and out of Jackson Hole might not be as easy as she'd like to imagine.

Drake wouldn't be in town much longer, either. He and Tracy had decided to move to Virginia. Drake planned to establish an equine rescue facility for Thoroughbred racehorses, and Tracy had just been admitted to the University of Virginia and had been able to transfer some of her online credits in psychology. Jeannette looked forward to visiting them.

Flying to Jackson Hole involved a much bigger commitment though. And then there was the issue of Zach. She couldn't come to Shoshone and pretend Zach didn't live here, too. She'd be looking for him around every corner. She'd want to know whether he'd found the woman of his dreams.

Ugh. That was a depressing thought. Yet he was a virile, lovable man who deserved to have a woman in his life. Once she left town, he'd probably start looking for someone who fancied a cabin in the woods.

As if her thoughts had drawn him to her, he approached the group of women gathered around a picnic table, a group she'd become a part of in the past half hour. She was proud of that, but she was glad to see Zach. She'd missed him.

"I don't want to interrupt," he said, "but the guitar players are tuning up and I'd like to borrow Jeannette for a dance."

Morgan laughed. "If the dancing's about to start, we'll all be out there, even the kids. A Last Chance party is about the food and the dancing." She turned to Lily. "Speaking of that, aren't you and Regan supposed to start this thing off?"

"I think that's a wedding tradition, not an engagement party tradition." Lily shrugged. "But what do I know? I've never been engaged before, let alone married."

"Regan and Lily probably should start the dancin'," Jeannette said. Then she realized maybe she shouldn't have stated that so directly. "At least that's how we do it in Virginia. Y'all might do it differently out here."

"See, I thought that was how it should go." Morgan made a shooing motion with her hands. "Go get your man, Lily, and boogie on out there so the rest of us can join in. My dancing feet are itching to see some action."

"Okay." Lily left her seat. "But don't leave us out there alone for too long, please. Regan and I are kind of new to this Last Chance dancing tradition. Compared to you guys, we might suck."

"Hey," Tyler said, "if my hubby can learn to hang with these folks, anybody can. You'll be fine." She glanced at Zach. "I'll bet Jack asked if you could dance when he hired you. Am I right?"

"You would be right."

"And can you?" Morgan asked.

"I should be able to manage, at least for a number or two."

Morgan looked doubtful. "We're talking about country swing, not hip-hop. Isn't that mostly what they do over in L.A.?"

"There's a fair amount of that, sure. But along the way I picked up a little country swing."

Jeannette wondered if anyone else caught the gleam in Zach's eyes as he said that. She'd spent enough time with him to know that expression meant he relished the challenge of whatever activity was coming up next, whether it was dancing or making love. And if he danced the way he made love, he'd be amazing at it.

She got up from the table and turned to Morgan and Tyler. "Thanks for the conversation. It's always fun to talk about travel plans."

Morgan smiled. "I'm glad we got to know you a little better."

"Me, too." Tyler stood and held out her hand. "Be sure and send me a postcard if you get to Dubrovnik. It's a cool little city."

"I will. Thanks." Jeannette squeezed Tyler's hand. "See you both on the dance floor."

As she walked away with Zach, he leaned closer. "Feeling better about the O'Connelli sisters?"

"Those two, for sure. Lily deserves the credit. She broke the ice, and believe me, there was some ice that needed to be broken."

"Lily's great, isn't she? From what I hear, she could have chosen to make a lot of money designing computer games up in Silicon Valley, but instead she

decided to operate an equine rescue facility in Shoshone."

"That's admirable." Jeannette could see why Zach
would be all in favor of a move like that. "Did she like
designing computer games?"

"I think she liked it okay, but it didn't satisfy her
the way the horse operation does."

"Then I'm glad she found what works for her. It's
so important to enjoy what you do."

"Absolutely."

If they'd been alone instead of heading for the
dance floor, she might have used that as a jumping-off
point for a discussion about the Wyoming bar-exam
study guide he'd bought. But this wasn't the time or
place for that.

The pair of guitarists opened with a Tim McGraw
number that didn't seem too taxing for Regan and Lily
as they two-stepped around the dance floor. Jeannette
couldn't remember ever dancing much when she'd
dated Regan, but he seemed to be having a great time.
Lily brought out his playful side. Apparently she and
Regan had been too much alike to cause sparks to fly.

Jeannette had been taught ballroom dancing as a
debutante, and the dance instructor had added a few
lessons in country swing for the fun of it. Watching
Regan and Lily confirmed that she'd be fine out there.
The catchy music had her tapping her toe.

She leaned toward Zach. "Those guitarists are
good. Who are they?"

"Two of the ranch hands."

"They're not professionals?"

"Not officially, although they've made some demos

and something might come of that. I've sent some tracks to a few of my friends in the business."

"That's terrific, Zach. Sometimes all it takes is the right connections."

"The thing is, they both love working on this ranch. I don't know if either of them really wants to perform full-time. Tyler sings with them sometimes, and I know she's not interested in living that life."

"Yes, but they're *good*. If they have the talent, then—"

"Not everyone wants to take it to the next level."

She didn't want to argue that point. She didn't want to argue at all, in fact. "So what are their names?" She was curious in case someday one of them became famous.

"Watkins is the older guy with the handlebar mustache. He has a first name, but nobody uses it. Trey Wheeler's the younger one. He's engaged to Elle, that blonde standing across the platform from us."

Jeannette located the woman he was talking about. Tall and athletic-looking, she was dressed like everyone else in jeans and a casual shirt. But there was nothing casual in the way she focused on Trey playing that guitar. "She's crazy about him. She's practically glowing with pride. That's very cute."

"He's crazy about her, too. She's a ski instructor at one of the resorts. Trey said this is the first summer she's stayed in Jackson Hole instead of flying down to Argentina to work during their winter months. Obviously she didn't want to leave him to go down there."

"Obviously." Jeannette couldn't help thinking there was a subtext to all the information Zach had given her about people who'd changed their lives for the sake of love.

She also wondered if Elle missed skiing while she stayed here to be with Trey. Sure, couples sometimes had to make sacrifices in order to be together. Would she? If Zach asked her to leave Virginia to be with him, would she consider it?

The answer wasn't simple. She wouldn't give up practicing law to be with him, and she couldn't imagine working in a law office every day and coming home to someone who had turned his back on that profession. Sooner or later that would become an issue between them.

They had to talk about it, and postponing that discussion weighed heavier with every passing moment. She took a deep breath to release some of her tension. The scent of recently cut lumber was strong here, and she guessed by the unmarred surface of the plywood platform that this had been the project that Zach had helped with this afternoon.

That thought reminded her that he still hadn't had any sleep. Until he had, she couldn't pester the poor guy with questions about his future. She leaned closer. "How are you holdin' up?"

"Great."

"I just happened to think…do you have to work tomorrow?"

"Yeah. I'm a new hire, so I work Sundays."

"At dawn?"

He chuckled. "That's when the animals get up."

"Whew. Then let's not stay long. I'm surprised you're upright, now that I think about it. Do you need coffee?"

"Dancing with you will be way more effective than caffeine for jump-starting my engine."

She smiled up at him. "What a nice thing to say."

"What a nice thing to do." He glanced at the dance floor. "More folks are joining in. Let's go." He took her hand and led her up the steps.

"What about my hat? Should I take it off?"

"Not unless you want to. I can work around your hat."

"Then I'll leave it on." She was pleased with the white straw hat and felt more country wearing it.

Anticipation raced through her at the prospect of dancing with Zach. She remembered how much she used to love dancing, but she hadn't made it a priority in a long while. She'd concentrated on work and forgotten how to relax.

Zach drew her into his arms, and from the moment he started to move, she knew dancing with him would be wonderful. He had an excellent sense of rhythm and dear God, did he know how to lead. His partner could be a mediocre dancer and Zach would make her look as if she should be a contestant on *Dancing with the Stars*.

As they circled the floor and he twirled her first one way and then another, she laughed from the sheer joy of it. She'd never had this much fun dancing with a guy. The song ended, and she gazed up at him, breathless with pleasure. "I know you must be tired, but can we do that once more?"

His grin flashed. "Yes, ma'am, we sure can."

"You're very good at this."

"You inspire me."

She met his gaze. "I think we inspire each other."

His expression grew serious as he brushed a thumb tenderly over her cheek. "Hold that thought."

Then the music began again and they were off, dancing together as if they'd been doing it for years. Yet she knew it was Zach making it seem that way. He was far more talented than he'd let on.

Other dancers called out encouragement and praise. Jeannette had never danced with someone who took such control of the floor, and it was a heady experience. Jack and Josie Chance whirled by and Jack gave them a thumbs-up.

"Looks like I won't lose my job for being a washout at dancing," Zach murmured.

"You were never in danger of that, were you?" She ducked under his arm as he turned her in another perfect spin.

He caught her expertly around the waist. "Nope. I won a couple of country swing dance competitions last year."

"You sandbagger!"

"Keep that under your hat." He guided her through another tricky maneuver.

"I will. Your secrets are safe with me."

He twirled her again and pulled her in close. "My secrets aren't my biggest concern."

She spun out and came back in tight against him. "What is?"

"My heart."

That left her speechless. They finished the dance, but those words, spoken casually, echoed between them. She didn't think they'd been meant casually at all.

Still trying to catch her breath from the pace of the

dance, she flattened her palms against his chest and felt the rapid beat of his heart, the one he was hoping would be safe with her. This temporary relationship didn't feel so temporary now. Lifting her gaze, she looked into eyes filled with intensity. "We should go."

"Yes, we should."

"We need to make the rounds and say goodbye."

"Absolutely."

Together they satisfied that obligation. They spoke with Lily and Regan before moving on to Morgan and her husband, Gabe. They caught Tyler right before she went up to sing, and Jeannette apologized for leaving without hearing her.

Everyone knew that Zach had to work in the morning, so no one expressed surprise that they were heading out. Jeannette could sense their quiet speculation, though. No doubt many of them had noticed the bond developing and wondered what would happen when she left for Virginia.

Last of all they searched out Jack and Josie. The Chances were conveniently talking with Jack's mother, Sarah, so they could thank her, too. Elegant without seeming formal, Sarah was dressed in jeans and a tailored shirt. She wore her silver hair in a simple pageboy and favored Native American jewelry.

As they were starting to move away, Sarah laid a hand on Jeannette's arm. "As I recall, tomorrow's your last day here."

"That's right." Jeannette fought the sinking feeling that statement brought.

"Zach will be tied up all day, of course, and you may want to spend the time enjoying his campsite. It's beautiful out there, but if you'd like to take a ride tomorrow afternoon, I'd be happy to show you around the property. On horseback is really the only way to see it."

Jeannette couldn't have been more surprised if Sarah had announced she'd be performing a fan dance later on in the evening. Everyone acknowledged Sarah Chance as the reigning queen of Shoshone, including a wide swath of countryside surrounding the little town. To be invited on a trail ride with her was almost like being granted an audience at Buckingham Palace.

A person didn't turn down an invitation like that. A Southern-born woman like Jeannette most certainly didn't. "I would love to," she said. "What time would you like me to come over?"

"Around two would be perfect. You're probably used to an English saddle, but would a Western one be okay for a couple of hours?"

"I'm sure it would. I'll be here. Thank you, that will be a perfect thing for my last day."

"I thought it might." Sarah held out her hand. "Until then."

As Jeannette took the older woman's hand, she felt the steely determination in that grip. Regan had told her all about Sarah Chance. The woman was a survivor. She'd lost her husband five years ago, but she'd carried on with the help of her three sons. Then she'd found a new love, Peter Beckett, and they'd married the previous summer.

Jeannette had no idea why Sarah had invited her on a trail ride, but the outing could prove to be educational. As Jeannette plotted out her future, which

had changed dramatically since the events of the previous Christmas, she was more than willing to soak
up wisdom wherever she could find it.

13

ON THE WAY back to the Airstream, Zach thought of all he wanted to say to Jeannette, but he wasn't sure how to say it or even if he should try. He'd already been fairly certain he was falling for her, but holding her in his arms while they danced had clinched it for him. She seemed to feel the same way, judging from the way her eyes had sparkled and her cheeks had flushed with pleasure.

Regan's words kept running through his head. *Depends on how much she wants to be with you.* That was the part that worried him. They'd had a great time together, but he didn't know if that was enough to offset her desire to stay with the Virginia law firm and make her parents proud.

They rode back with the windows down, and because the road was rough, he had to take it slow. Night sounds filtered into the truck's cab. Crickets chirped from the bushes along the roadside and occasionally the hoot of an owl would drift from the nearby woods. The wolves were quiet tonight, but he heard the yip of coyotes.

"I guess you know how much I like it here," he said at last.

"I do, and I understand. It's beautiful."

He wasn't sure how to take that. Everyone said Jackson Hole was beautiful, but not everyone was willing to move there so they could soak up that beauty year-round. He had no idea how to begin this conversation. How in the hell could he ask her to give up everything to come out here and start over?

Finally he decided to wait until they got back to the Airstream. But he wouldn't broach the subject while they were in bed together. That wasn't fair. He wouldn't use the passion they shared to influence her to say something tonight that she'd regret in the morning.

Maybe he should just make love to her, go to sleep and tackle this tomorrow. That would be far more logical, except that he wasn't in the mood to be logical. He used to pride himself on his practical thinking, but emotion and exhaustion had him by the throat right now and he needed some idea of where he stood with her.

"I have a couple of folding chairs stashed under the trailer," he said. "Would you like to sit outside for a little while? Maybe we'll hear the wolves again."

"That sounds nice."

He loved the way she said the word *nice* with a long *i* sound instead of a short one. Now every time he heard a woman with a Southern accent, he'd think of Jeannette. Hell, every time he heard wolves howl, he'd think of her, and every time he danced the two-step, and every time he ate a club sandwich or watched *Sabrina*.

Except he wouldn't watch that movie again if she left for good. That was one thing he could eliminate from his life to decrease the pain. He might give up club sandwiches, too, and champagne. But that wouldn't be enough to mute the effect of losing her. He'd have to sell the Airstream.

When he thought of how she'd burrowed into his life in such a short time, he swallowed a groan of dismay. Somehow he had to convince her that she belonged with him. The alternative—that she would leave and he'd never see her again—was unacceptable.

He pulled into the campsite, shut off the engine and climbed out of the cab. She was out before he made it around to the other side. And then suddenly he was holding her, because he couldn't help it.

"I don't want you to leave." The words came out before he could stop them. "I want to find a way for us to be together."

She held on tight, her voice muffled against his chest. "Then we have to talk about something I found in your trailer. I'd meant to put it off until you got some sleep, but I guess we have to do this now."

He drew back to stare at her in the pale light of the moon. "Something you found in my trailer? What in God's name could that be?"

"The study guide for passing the Wyoming bar."

"What?" He laughed in disbelief. "Why would you want to talk about that?"

"I need to know why you bought it."

It was a perfectly good question, though he didn't have a neat answer. "I don't know. It doesn't matter. Listen, Regan said something tonight that got me to thinking, and I—"

"It does matter, Zach. What made you buy that study guide?"

He realized she'd push until he offered an explanation. That wouldn't come easily, because he'd never examined his motivation for buying the book. "I suppose I thought of it as a backup plan." He looked into her face, which was mostly in shadows.

"I found it while I was browsing through your bookshelf looking for something to read."

"I haven't really looked at it."

"I could see that. But when I found it, I had this crazy idea that you hadn't totally given up on practicing law."

"Actually, I have." He could guess that wasn't what she wanted to hear, but he wanted them to be straight with each other. "I bought that not long after I moved here. I got hired on at the Last Chance, but Jack gave me a two-week trial before he put me on permanently. I loved it here so much that I figured if Jack fired me, I would study for the bar and work as an attorney if I had to, just so I could stay in Jackson Hole."

"Then you never intend to get back into it?"

He rubbed the small of her back. How he loved touching her, and he could feel that privilege slipping away. "I'm afraid of what practicing law does to me. Once I step into that world, I could get sucked back into a frame of mind where I have to be the best. I was so damned competitive, Jeannette. I kept score with materialistic things. I don't ever want to be that person again."

"Do you think I'm like that?"

"No. No! I'm not condemning you or what you

do. It's me that has the problem with the profession, not you."

"But you're in a different environment now, and you've had that revelation." She gazed up at him. "Surely it would be different here."

He sighed. "And if it's not, I've poisoned the well. I've ruined what I love about being here. I don't want to risk it. The peace of mind I've found working at the Last Chance is like nothing I've ever known before."

"Zach, I really think—"

"What about this? What if you started a law practice in Shoshone? Regan said the town could really use one. I know what I'm asking. You're about to make partner, and you've spent years working for it, but..." His throat tightened. "I want you to stay. I'm trying to come up with a way it might work for you."

"But you see, it wouldn't." Her soft words cut deeper than any knife possibly could.

The rejection hit hard. Her reasons might only make that rejection worse, but he had to have them spelled out, anyway. "Is it because you don't want to give up your practice in Virginia?"

"That's part of it."

"If it's a money issue, I could back you while you get established here."

"I'm not worried about the money. I've saved, too. Not as much as you, but I could ride out the lean times until I built up a client list."

"I don't suppose your parents would like the idea of you moving out here."

She hesitated. "No, probably not."

"Is that the problem?"

She slipped out of his arms and walked a few feet

away. "My relationship with them is...complicated. I'm sure you've figured that out. Since being in Jackson Hole, and specifically spending time with you, I've started looking at things differently. I thank you for that. But my problems with my parents aren't what's standing in the way of us being together."

"Then what is?"

She turned to face him. "You are."

"Me? I'm trying to find a solution so we *can* be together!"

"But without changing anything in your life. I'd do all the changing."

He rubbed the back of his neck. She had a point. "Are you thinking I should offer to move back there?"

"Although that would be imminently fair, I wouldn't ask it of you. Ironically, you're more attached to this place than I am to Virginia." She took a deep breath. "I'll admit it might be good for me to put some distance between me and my parents. I love them, but that doesn't mean I should live in the same town with them."

Hope surged anew. "I'm glad to hear you say that."

"But neither should I live in the same town with you."

"Why the hell not?"

"Because you have a fine legal mind, and you're about to let it rot. I realize that's your privilege, but I don't want to be around to see that happen."

His emotions were all over the place, but the one that shouldered its way forward at the moment was anger. "You're making this far more dramatic than it is. People switch jobs all the time. No big deal."

"It is if all you're doing is runnin' away from yourself."

His jaw tightened. "That's not how I see it."

"What if your services as a lawyer would be useful to this community? You said yourself that Regan thinks Shoshone could use a lawyer. How about you?"

"And give up what I'm doing now?"

"You wouldn't have to. You could manage both. Your ability with legal issues is exceptional, whether you admit it or not. I could tell that even with the short discussion we had on the way to Jackson."

He gazed at her in silence.

"You have a gift, Zach. Maybe you didn't use that gift wisely in L.A. Maybe you let circumstances control you instead of takin' control yourself. I've heard that the Last Chance Ranch helps people work through that kind of issue."

"Exactly. And that's what I love about the place. I figured out that I'm happy working as a ranch hand. It suits me fine."

She regarded him quietly. "I'm sure it does, for now. If you stick with this program, it'll suit you better and better, I suppose. Eventually your legal knowledge will become outdated and maybe you'll even lose your analytical edge because you're not sharpenin' it on a regular basis. But you used to love that analytical work, didn't you?"

"A long time ago. Before I let the glitz and glamour get the best of me."

"Do you hear yourself? You *let* that happen. You don't have to let it happen again. It's more temptin' to be a hotshot when you're twenty-five than when you're thirty-five."

"I don't know about that. Look at that big-ass truck I bought."

"Damn it, Zach! You're like a dog with a bone. You are capable of making different choices this time around!"

He took off his hat and tunneled his fingers through his hair. "You don't understand what you're asking of me."

"Oh, yes I do. I'm askin' you to be true to who you are, to embrace all sides of yourself."

"What if I'm supposed to be a ranch hand? Because I'm telling you, this job fits me like a glove. I'm happy to drive to the ranch every day. The working conditions are great. I don't have to wear fancy clothes and I love being around horses."

"But I also listened to you throwing out creative ideas for handlin' my case. You cited legal precedent from memory. I knew then I'd met a lawyer who spends time as a ranch hand, not a ranch hand who dabbles in the law."

"And you accuse *me* of being stubborn. You've got it in your head that practicing law is my destiny and you won't rest until I agree to do it!"

She sighed. "Actually, the defense rests as of now. I can see we're not gettin' anywhere. We're both tired. And you probably need to think some more about this."

He opened his mouth to say that he didn't have to think about anything. He loved ranch work and that was what he intended to do for the foreseeable future.

"I would save my rebuttal if I were you, counselor."

In spite of the tense situation, that made him smile. "Why?"

"Because you really do need to take a recess and give yourself a chance to think about the evidence I've presented. In the meantime, I have a suggestion for what we can do during that recess."

His startled laughter woke some birds in a nearby tree and they fluttered restlessly. "Are you saying what I think you are?"

"That I want to go inside and make love? Yes, I do."

"I thought we were fighting."

"Debatin'."

"Whatever. We sure as hell aren't agreeing on anything. I doubt sex will change that, either."

"It won't." She said it matter-of-factly. "But it'll be fun and relaxin'. Then we can get some sleep and review the situation tomorrow."

"I don't know what kind of lawyer I was." He closed the gap between them and drew her into his arms. "But I can testify that you're an excellent one."

"Thank you." She wound her arms around his neck. "If I do say so myself, I am. Now let's get movin', cowboy."

They made it inside the Airstream in record time and left a trail of clothes on their way back to the bedroom. Zach leaned against the wall and got rid of his boots before helping Jeannette tug hers off. They each shucked their jeans and underwear and tumbled naked and laughing onto the double bed.

Holding her felt so amazing. Kissing her was the second-best activity he'd ever known. Then he rolled on a condom and settled into the best activity ever. When his cock was buried deep in her warmth, all was right in his world.

Pausing to savor the moment, he looked into her

green eyes. "You sure are something, Jeannette Trenton."

She smiled as she ran her hands down his back to clutch his hips. "So are you, Zach Powell."

"Not every woman would invite a man to bed under these circumstances."

"I'm not every woman."

"No, you're certainly not." He leaned down and kissed her with all the longing in his heart as he began to love her with slow, sure strokes.

She answered his kiss and she answered the urging of his body as she rose to meet each firm thrust. They were so good together. Their disagreement faded until there was only this…sweet friction creating mutual pleasure.

As his breathing quickened, he lifted his mouth from hers. She moaned and pressed her fingertips into the small of his back. "I'm close," she murmured.

"I know." He shifted his angle and increased the pace as she tightened around his aching cock. "I can feel it." He'd ride out her orgasm so he could give her a second one. Then he'd claim his own.

Gasping, she arched upward, on the brink of surrender. "Come with me."

"No." But apparently his body had other ideas, because it clenched in readiness. "You deserve more than one—"

"Please."

He struggled to hold back. "Not yet."

"But this feels so *right*." She began to pant. "I want you with me. Please let go!"

Her desperate plea snapped his control. With a deep groan, he pounded into her, unleashing his passion with a ferocity that shocked him. What had begun as a friendly roll in the hay had transformed into something far more intense.

Squeezing his eyes shut, he came in a rush while her climax rolled over his pulsing cock. Gasping, he cried out her name and shuddered against her, caught in a whirlpool of sensation that rivaled anything he'd known.

When he stopped shaking, when at last he could draw a steady breath, he opened his eyes and gazed down at her. "That was…" He had no words.

"I know." Her expression was tender as she cupped his face in both hands. "I know."

Earlier tonight he'd suspected the stakes were going up in this relationship. Now he found himself looking into the eyes of the only woman he would ever want by his side. The stakes had just shot through the roof.

14

JEANNETTE WOKE TO bright sunshine, the sound of birds outside the open window and a hastily scribbled note on Zach's pillow. The down pillow—of course he would have bought the best—retained the impression of his head, but it was cool to the touch. Jeannette glanced at the clock and realized he'd been gone for hours.

Had to leave for work, the note said. *Will be back after 5. Z.* Using only his initial suggested a certain intimacy, but he hadn't added a closing endearment or even *XXOO.* Had she been the one writing the note to him, she would have had trouble with a closing, too.

Thinking that she loved him after such a short time sounded delusional. Yet she couldn't come up with any other word that described the bone-deep emotion that gripped her whenever she thought of Zach. She cared in a way that couldn't be explained given their brief acquaintance.

Sure, the sex had been great from the beginning, and they'd had a lot of it. But it had never been only about sex, although she'd tried to tell herself that. The term *making love* wasn't a euphemism in this case, at least not for her.

She'd felt a deeper connection from the moment they'd met in the barn. She'd always prided herself on being logical, but the feelings that had developed so quickly between them defied common sense. She sensed that Zach might be struggling with the same question of emotion versus logic.

Glancing at the clock, she was shocked to discover it was after ten. Normally she was too type A to sleep this late, especially in a strange bed. Zach must have left with the stealth of a cat burglar, which was amazing considering his size and the tight quarters. He'd even managed to open some windows without making noise.

She could picture him taking great care not to disturb her, though. She wondered if he'd set a mental alarm clock in order to wake up on time. She could have done that, too, but she'd had no obligation other than her ride with Sarah at two, so she hadn't bothered.

The concept of leisure was foreign to her, but apparently she'd adapted well enough to sleep late this morning. Stretching languidly, she climbed out of bed, pulled on Zach's enormous bathrobe and padded into the living room. Once again, Zach had picked up the discarded clothes. Hers were folded neatly on the living room couch.

Rainbows danced on the wall. She peered out the window. Something moved in the trees, and a thrill of apprehension zipped up her spine until she identified the shapes of deer.

She counted three as they moved through the trees,

no doubt headed down to the stream for a drink. If she lived in a cabin in the woods, she'd be treated to sightings of wildlife on a regular basis. More than that, her growing self-reliance would be nurtured in a setting like this.

Standing in the living room of Zach's Airstream, she came to a decision—and a pretty darned big one, too. She wanted to leave Virginia, regardless of how her relationship with Zach turned out. Whether she'd end up here was a question mark, but she needed a complete change of scenery and some geographical distance from her parents.

She wasn't sure how much their expectations ruled her behavior, but she suspected it was a lot. Whenever she'd thought of the partnership she'd been working so hard for, she'd imagined how pleased they'd be. The partnership had been a prize to lay at their feet, not something she craved for herself.

Without this trip to Jackson Hole and meeting Zach, she might never have gained that insight. Ironically, watching him avoid his issues had brought hers into sharper contrast. She might be able to retain her budding feeling of independence without moving, but changing her environment would help enormously. If she stayed there, she might fall back into old, familiar patterns.

Which was exactly why Zach didn't want to practice law. She sucked in a quick breath. Okay, she got it now. He'd made changes in his life, changes he didn't want to reverse. He was afraid practicing law might coax him into old habits.

Although she could look at the man he was now and be certain that wouldn't happen, he couldn't see that. Telling him he'd be fine working as a lawyer wouldn't convince him any more than someone telling her that she'd function just as well living a few miles away from her parents' horse farm. She'd rather play it safe and leave. Zach would rather play it safe and be a ranch hand.

Of course their situations weren't identical. She'd always be her parents' daughter, which meant she had to deal with those dynamics even if she were living somewhere else. Zach had completely severed his ties with his profession, something he'd once loved and probably still did on some level. There was the rub.

Groaning in frustration, she sank down to the small couch in his living room. Understanding him didn't make the problems go away. If anything, they seemed more daunting than ever. She'd thought to use lawyerly logic on him, but that wasn't going to do a damn bit of good.

After another leisurely breakfast of coffee and PB-and-J sandwiches, she cleaned up the kitchen and made Zach's bed. Taking plenty of time for these simple chores felt relaxing, but she could feel the beginnings of restlessness.

She texted Erin to find out how her research was going but didn't get an immediate answer. Maybe Erin was taking a few hours off. After all, it was Sunday. But Jeannette had been away from work for more than a week, and she missed it.

Hoping that Erin would see the text and respond, she paged through a couple of magazines. Finally she gave up and navigated the challenge of Zach's tiny indoor shower. She dressed in another pair of her recently purchased jeans and a short-sleeved knit top.

Her boots hadn't rubbed blisters on her feet and the white straw hat would be perfect for riding. She felt like a Westerner, although a slightly bored Westerner. Thank goodness Sarah had invited her for a ride. And she should be back before Zach came home.

Then she realized that if she locked the door behind her as she'd planned to, she didn't have a key to get back in. She checked around the outside for a hidden spare and didn't find one. Oh, well. Zach was at the ranch, so she'd find him there and ask to borrow the key.

With that problem solved, she climbed into her rental car and headed slowly and carefully back to the ranch. She drove straight down to the barn, where Sarah was already saddling the smaller of two brown-and-white Paints. Jeannette parked and walked over to help.

"You're right on time!" Sarah called out.

"I've been lookin' forward to it." She approached the larger of the two horses. "Want me to go ahead and saddle this guy?"

"Sure. I picked Spilled Milk for you, so you might as well get to know each other. He's partial to women so you two should do fine together."

"I'm sure we will. You're a handsome boy, Spilled Milk." Jeannette copied Sarah's saddling technique. The process was similar to what she was used to with an English saddle, so she probably could have muddled through on her own. Truthfully she hadn't saddled her own horse in a while, but she'd learned as a kid and the process came back quickly.

A groom had always saddled a horse for Jeannette's mother whenever she rode, and Jeannette had fallen into that habit, too. Saddling Spilled Milk herself did allow her to become acquainted with the horse, just as Sarah had said. A scratch under his mane, a pat on his withers and some murmured words of greeting made a huge difference in how she felt about the up-coming ride. Wherever she moved would definitely be horse country and from now on she'd personally saddle any horse she rode.

After she tightened the cinch, she mounted up to check the length of the stirrups. "These seem a little long," she said to Sarah. "But I'm used to the shorter ones of an English saddle, so you'd better tell me if this is right or not."

"They look fine to me. When you stand up in them, you should have a little daylight between you and the saddle, but not a whole lot. Yeah, that's perfect. Ready?"

"You bet. Can't wait."

Sarah climbed on her horse. "Then we're off. In the beginning the trail's wide enough for us to ride side-by-side, which makes it easier to talk."

Jeannette walked Spilled Milk down a path that led through a meadow filled with the buzzing of in-sects and a riot of red, yellow and purple wildflowers. Breathing deep, she savored the familiar scent of horse and oiled leather. Tension flowed out as she exhaled, and she vowed to spend more time with horses in the future. They never failed to relax her.

Sarah rode alongside on her dramatically marked brown-and-white Paint. The mare carried herself like royalty, arching both her neck and her tail as she pranced more than walked down the trail.

"Pretty mare."

Sarah patted her horse's neck with obvious affection. "This is Bertha Mae."

"Bertha Mae?" Jeannette laughed. "Lookin' at her I would have guessed a far more exotic name than that."

"That's the name she arrived with, and nobody thought to change it. Now I wouldn't want to." She glanced over at Jeannette. "I don't know if you've heard that my first husband died in a rollover with a horse trailer."

"Regan told me about it. That must have been a terrible time for your family."

"It was. Really terrible. But we all came through it, including Bertha Mae."

"She was the horse in the trailer?"

Sarah nodded. "At first I wanted nothing to do with her. Nobody did, although it wasn't her fault, poor girl."

"No, but it's understandable that you wouldn't want to be around her." The squeak of leather and the buzz of insects created a comforting background that seemed to invite confidences.

"Eventually I started going out to the barn to talk to her," Sarah continued, "which helped me and probably helped her. She had to have been lonesome, although she wasn't as ostracized as I'd thought. Jack had secretly begun to work with her. Aside from being traumatized by the accident, she'd never been ridden."

"That's incredible." Jeannette gazed at the well-mannered horse. "You'd never guess that she'd been through all that."

"It was mostly Jack's doing. Four years ago he rode her in Gabe and Morgan's wedding ceremony, and she's been a wonderful saddle horse ever since. I love taking her out on the trail."

"What a heartwarmin' story. I'm glad you told me."

"I guess it's my way of illustrating how time can work wonders. I'm so encouraged by the healing that seems to have taken place between you, Regan and Drake. Thank you for placing yourself in what has sometimes been an uncomfortable situation."

Jeannette grinned at her. "Aw, 'twarn't nuthin', ma'am."

"Heaven help us, you're learning the lingo."

"Not really. That was straight out of a movie. But I feel more a part of the ranch after last night's party. This ride helps, too. I can't tell you how much I appreciate the invitation."

"Zach mentioned that you were comfortable around horses, so it seemed a shame not to take you out for a ride. How's that Western saddle treating you?"

Jeannette leaned back against the cantle. "It feels like an easy chair compared to what I'm used to, so I'll need to watch myself and make sure I don't nod off."

"Want to go a little faster?"

"Oh, no! I didn't mean to imply I was bored. Just very relaxed. Trust me, that's a good thing. I tend to be way too tense and driven."

"Then I'm glad I brought you out here before you have to head back to a more frantic pace."

"So am I." She thought of her recent decision to move and that it would logically take her out West. This ride through wildflowers on a warm August day, with the Grand Tetons still topped with last winter's snow, gave her a taste of what summer was like in Jackson Hole.

But the winter months were legendary for the bitter cold and blizzards that kept people indoors for days. She decided to get a woman's perspective on that. "How do you cope with winters here?"

Sarah gave her a curious glance before answering. "We concentrate on the cozy factor."

"Oh, really?" Jeannette laughed. "That sounds kind of fun."

"It is, although when the kids were toddlers I'd be lying if I didn't say there were days I wanted to tear my hair out. But you learn to be a family. When the electricity goes out and you're operating on generator power, you conserve that resource. Instead of watching TV or listening to music, you light candles, play board games, or…find other ways to amuse yourselves and keep warm."

From Sarah's tone, Jeannette knew exactly what she was talking about. "You make it sound romantic."

"It can be, especially with the right man. It helps to be very good friends with whoever shares your living space. Much as I loved Jonathan, my first husband, he had a tendency to get moody in the winter. Pete is the most optimistic and joyful person I know, even without one of those light boxes to counteract the lack of sun. I confess it's easier to be snowbound with Pete."

Jeannette thought about being snowbound with Zach. He'd probably be fine. "I'm afraid I'd be the one who'd go stir-crazy and cause problems," she said.

"You might surprise yourself." Sarah hesitated. "Are you contemplating a winter vacation in Jackson Hole?"

"Maybe." She didn't dare say more. Zach couldn't get wind of her plans to move. That would only add pressure to an already tense situation. If he ever decided to start a new legal practice, it needed to be for his sake and not because she'd dangled the possibility of her moving to Shoshone as an enticement.

"If you do, let me know. You're welcome anytime, and we usually have room except right before Christmas. We fill up with extended family then."

Jeannette gazed at her. "You have no idea how much that offer means to me. A few days ago I thought I'd never be accepted here."

"As I said, time can work wonders. I've been treading a fine line because I have a daughter-in-law who wasn't eager to be your friend."

"Morgan. I know. Thanks to Lily, I think Morgan and I could become friends."

"I think so, too. And then there's Tyler. She's like a daughter-in-law even though technically she's not. But the ice is cracking there, too."

"I'll need a bit more time to win over Cassidy."

"Yes." Sarah chuckled. "That little redhead is a spitfire. She sees everything in terms of black and white, but she'll mellow. If you come back this winter, I predict you'll make friends with Cassidy."

"I'd like that." She noticed that Sarah had made no mention of Zach or what the future might hold for the two of them. Sarah's generous invitation wasn't conditional on whether she continued to see Zach. Sarah was extending her friendship to her regardless of what happened with him.

That made the gesture even more precious. Apparently Sarah had decided that she was worthy of being included in activities at the Last Chance. She might not be family, but she was welcomed as a friend of the family. She was no longer a person to be shunned. That was a personal triumph.

Sarah gazed out at the wide path stretching ahead of them. "Are you *sure* you don't want to go faster? Spilled Milk has a lovely canter."

In her current jubilant mood, a canter across this meadow sounded excellent. "Let's go for it!"

In no time they were covering ground so fast that she had to clap a hand to her head to keep her hat from flying off. At last Sarah held up an arm and they slowed to a trot, and then a walk.

Sarah's cheeks were pink and she looked far younger than her sixty-nine years. Because she was an experienced trail rider, she'd secured her hat with a string under her chin. Jeannette had thought the string was too dorky, but next time she rode like this she'd use one.

Sarah turned Bertha Mae back in the direction they'd come. "Fun, huh?"

"Too much fun. I loved it."

"Think of us while you're back in Virginia. And do consider coming out sometime this winter. See how you like us when the snow's on the ground."

"Thanks. I will." She looked over at Sarah, and for the first time wondered if her hostess were indeed playing matchmaker. If so, she had an extremely subtle touch. And it was working.

15

AT SOME POINT during the day Zach remembered that Sarah had invited Jeannette for a ride and there would be a problem with the key to the Airstream. He removed it from his key ring and tucked it in his other pocket. He'd make sure he got it to her one way or another.

As it turned out, he was involved in stacking sections of the new platform in the tractor barn at the time Sarah and Jeannette were scheduled to ride out, so he missed her. But after he finished working on that project, a job that left him hot and sweaty, he walked outside and spotted Jeannette's rental car parked near the barn.

The sight of it there made his pulse leap, which indicated just how far gone he was. He didn't even have to see her. A glimpse of her rental car was enough to make his heart beat faster. He was a sorry mess, and he had less than twenty-four hours to sort things out.

Or maybe he had more than twenty-four hours. He might have twenty-five or -six. He wasn't exactly sure when her plane left. He should have asked, but he hadn't realized how critical every minute would be-come. Because he wanted to maximize his time with her, he wanted to have a few hours off tomorrow until she had to leave for the airport. He'd need to ask for that today and hope Jack would give it to him.

Wednesday was normally his free day, so if he could switch it to Monday, he'd be all set. Even after a month of having a boss, he still hadn't adjusted to the idea of accounting for his time. Every so often he'd chafe at the concept that he couldn't leave when he chose to do so. He'd spent too many years in charge of his own calendar, and now he was working a speci-fied shift.

Not that he was complaining about that. God, no. He loved ranch work and was grateful for the oppor-tunity Jack was providing. Even if switching his day off wasn't possible, coming in after she left for the airport shouldn't be a big deal. He wasn't exactly a key man around here.

That didn't bother him, either. It was comforting to be a cog in a wheel for a change instead of the whole damned wheel with overhead up the wazoo. He was glad he no longer had an office full of employees who depended on him to bring in the big bucks.

So what if he felt a little prick of irritation when he had to ask for time off? It was a small price to pay for the peace of mind he'd gained by downsizing his life. He'd done the right thing, no matter what Jean-nette thought about it. She couldn't see things from his perspective right now, but eventually she might.

As luck would have it, Jack Chance, his boss, hap-pened to pull up in his cherry-red truck. Zach decided that red worked way better than black in this environment. Anyone who had grown up here would know that, but he was from L.A. and had spent his life driving on freeways. He still had much to learn about the cowboy way.

He walked over to the truck as Jack climbed down from the cab. "If you have a minute, I need to ask you something."

Jack shut the door of the cab. "What's that?"

"I'd like time off tomorrow so I can stay at the campsite until Jeannette leaves for the airport."

"I think that can be arranged. When does she leave?"

Here came the embarrassing part. He should have checked it in advance. When he was in the swing of things as a lawyer, he always stayed up on details. "I'm not sure, but I figure middle of the day. She's flying east, so she'll lose time and won't want to arrive too late."

Jack nodded. "You have no idea what time her flight is, do you?"

"No, I don't."

"Hang on. Let's call somebody who might know." He consulted his phone and punched a button. "Yeah, Drake, do you know what time Jeannette's flight leaves?" He paused. "That might be close enough. What airline did she come in on? Okay, thanks." He disconnected. "He thinks it's sometime between eleven and noon."

"That would make sense."

"I'll look online." Jack brought up a screen on his phone. "Here we go. I'll bet she's leaving on the eleven-fifteen out of Jackson Hole. That's the right airline, and the timing matches Drake's estimate."

"That's probably the one, but I'll confirm it with her."

Jack gazed at him. "Yeah, do that. But you might as well take the whole day off and then work Wednesday instead."

"Okay. Thanks."

"No problem." Jack continued to study him. "How's everything going?"

"We have the new platform stowed."

"I mean with Jeannette, brainiac. Did you suggest that she might want to come back here and start a law firm?"

"I did."

"And what was her reaction?"

Zach didn't want to have this conversation but it couldn't be avoided without refusing to discuss it. After the interest Jack had taken that seemed rude. "She thinks the person opening the law firm should be me."

"Oh, really? And while you play legal eagle, is she gonna put up preserves and crochet afghans?"

Picturing that very un-Jeannette scenario made him laugh. "Hardly." But he hadn't considered what might happen if he did what she wanted and started practicing law in Shoshone. "It doesn't matter. I don't want to get back into law."

"Oh." Jack tipped back his hat. "And what does she think of that?"

"Don't know yet. Either she accepts my decision and decides to open an office here, or she disagrees with me and decides to stay in Virginia as a result." He was proud of the calm way he laid out those two alternatives, even though option number two made his stomach clench.

"Any idea how it'll go?"

"Hell, I don't know. Last night she made it clear that she doesn't want to be with me unless I…how did she describe it? I'm supposed to *use my gift*. She thinks I was put on this earth to be a lawyer. I think that's bull. I'm hoping she backs down from that position, but if not, she'll stay in Virginia because I have no intention of practicing law again."

Jack blew out a breath. "If she stays back East, it will suck for you, but it will also suck for me."

"Why?"

"Well, I wasn't going to bring this up and muddy the waters, but old Barnaby Hanks, who's handled ranch legal issues ever since I can remember, is retiring and moving to Florida."

"So what? He must be transferring his clients to someone."

"Oh, yeah, some guy in Jackson, and I guess I can deal with that, but I'm spoiled. I'm used to having my lawyer right here in town. True, he's been threatening to retire for years and I think we're his only remaining client, so I get why he wants to leave, but I don't have to like it."

"How long have you known about this upcoming retirement?"

Jack tugged his hat back down so it shaded his eyes. "Oh, a while."

"More than a month?"

"Maybe."

"Did you hire me with the idea I might come in handy when this guy retired?"

Jack shrugged. "It's possible that such a thing crossed my mind. And then Jeannette blew into town and you two became chummy, so I got all excited at the prospect of having *two* lawyers on hand. Now it seems I might go from two to zero and I'm stuck with some stranger in Jackson."

"I never said I'd help you with your legal issues, Jack."

"I know you didn't."

"Besides, legally I couldn't without getting a license to practice in Wyoming, and I have no plans to do that."

"Maybe not right this minute you don't, but you're supersmart. You could get licensed in no time flat if you had to." Jack peered at him. "Couldn't you?"

"I don't know. But the question's moot because I don't plan on doing it. Now I have a question for you. You hired me for my potential legal advice but if I don't agree to take the bar exam, am I out of a job?"

"Hell, no. That's not how I operate, Powell. You've only been here a month, but you should know that I hired you as a ranch hand and as long as you do the job, you're welcome to stay. If you choose to get licensed in Wyoming, that would be a bonus, but if you don't want to, that's your choice."

Zach smiled in relief. "Glad to hear it. I wish Jeannette had the same attitude."

"So do I, because at least then she might decide to set up shop here. I also think you'd be a much happier cowboy if she agrees to hang around. But I'll work with what I've got."

"That's a good approach." Zach would do his

damnedest to adopt that approach in the next twenty-four hours.

"It's just that Barnaby and I would sit on the front porch of the ranch house and drink coffee or beer, depending on the time of day, and hash out whatever legal question had come up. He did the same with my dad. I have a tough time believing some guy will drive down from Jackson to hang out on the front porch with me."

Zach glanced over at the two-story log ranch house with its long covered porch lined with rockers. "I don't know, Jack. It's a hell of a front porch. I'd invite him down and see what happens."

"Frankly, I'd rather sit with you in one of those rockers. Are you *sure* you won't consider it? You'd have no trouble building a practice here. You could work fewer hours and make more money. Doesn't that tempt you at all?"

"Yes." Zach shoved his hands in his pockets and stared at the rugged profile of the Grand Tetons. "And that's what scares me."

"Scares you? I don't under—"

"We'll have to table this discussion." Zach watched two riders come toward them. "Your mother and Jeannette are back."

Jack turned. "So they are." He lowered his voice. "Maybe Mom softened her up some."

"Softened her up? Is your mother part of this campaign, too?"

"I wouldn't call it a campaign, exactly, but she's also angling for the two-lawyer solution."

"I hope to God she didn't mention that to Jeannette," Zach said in an undertone. He smiled and waved at the riders. "Jeannette might feel like she's being double-teamed."

"Mom wouldn't mention it. I warned her not to. I said the situation was still very tenuous."

"No shit."

Jack laughed. "Don't give up, brainiac." Then he raised his voice. "Welcome back, ladies! Have a good ride?"

"Great ride!" Jeannette's cheeks were flushed a becoming pink and her green eyes sparkled. "What a perfect day for it." She looked completely at home in the Western saddle.

Gazing up at her, Zach wished they'd met earlier. He could have taken her out riding last Wednesday. But if she agreed to move here, he'd work riding into his schedule on a regular basis.

He'd considered buying the little rental cabin that sat just outside the boundaries of the Last Chance. Drake had lived in it when he'd arrived from Virginia and Jeannette had stayed there for a couple of days before moving to the Bunk and Grub. If Zach bought it and Jeannette agreed to live there with him, they'd be close enough to take a couple of horses out on his day off. He'd considered buying his own horse, although that might be a bad idea now that he was working full-time.

"Zach?" Sarah's voice broke into his thoughts. "Would you mind taking Bertha Mae back to the barn for me? I promised Morgan I'd babysit the grandkids and I'd like to freshen up before they arrive."

"Be glad to. I can handle both of them if you like." He stepped forward and took hold of the mare's bridle in one hand and the gelding's in the other as the two women dismounted.

"If nobody minds," Jeannette said, "I'd like to unsaddle Spilled Milk and rub him down myself."

Sarah glanced at her with obvious approval. "I not only don't mind, but I'm glad you want to. It's the sign of a good horsewoman to take care of your own mount. Normally I do, but those grandkids will be here any minute."

"Then you'd better get goin'." Jeannette held out her hand. "Thank you so much for the ride. I loved it."

Sarah beamed as she clasped Jeannette's hand in both of hers. "It was fun, wasn't it? You'll just have to come back when you can stay longer. Believe it or not, we sometimes ride in the winter, too, if the snow's not too deep. And I've also been agitating for a sleigh."

Jack laughed. "And I'm looking into it, Mom. You aren't the only one agitating. Your grandchildren are all about the sleigh. I'm sure you've had nothing to do with that, though."

"Of course not." Sarah winked at Jeannette as she released her hand. "You have a safe flight home. Hope to see you back soon."

"I'd like that."

"So would I. Take care." With another warm smile, Sarah turned and hurried toward the house.

"That sleigh's going to be the death of me," Jack muttered. "I ordered it from a guy down in Cheyenne who specializes in 'em and he's taking for*ever* to make it. First he promised it by Labor Day. Now it's Halloween. It may actually show up next June."

"For one horse or two?" Jeannette asked.

"One. It'll be tricky enough to get one horse used

to the thing, let alone two. Besides, the holiday song is about a one-horse open sleigh, so that's what we're going for."

"She'll love it," Zach said.

Jeannette nodded in agreement. "She absolutely will. And the grandkids will go nuts over it. I would have when I was a little girl. Heck, I still love the idea."

Jack looked at her, his expression as warm as his mother's. "Then come out this winter and give it a whirl. I've ordered cozy lap robes and the harnesses will have bells on them."

"Sounds wonderful."

"It will be if that little old sleigh-maker gets the lead out. Listen, Zach, why don't you and Jeannette take care of the horses and head on back to your campsite after that? Stowing the platform in the tractor barn was my main objective for the day, so you might as well knock off a little early."

"Thanks." Zach was appreciative, but he was all too aware that he wouldn't have been allowed to leave without Jack's permission. He might need another few weeks to get past that and accept that he was paid to work a given number of hours per week. Only the boss could set his own hours, and the boss was no longer Zachary Powell.

He hadn't minded that so much when he hadn't had anything else to do. But having Jeannette here made a difference. He found himself wanting a little more freedom of movement.

Jack held out his hand to Jeannette. "I probably won't see you again before you fly out. I gave Powell the day off tomorrow so you two can spend a little time together before you drive to the airport."

"Thank you." Jeannette shook his hand. "I've enjoyed myself here. I can see why Regan talked about the ranch so much, and I'm glad I finally was able to see it."

"The door's always open."

"I'll remember that. Goodbye, Jack."

"I prefer *until we meet again*." He smiled and touched the brim of his black Stetson before heading off toward the ranch house.

Jeannette gazed after him with a bemused smile. "He sure is rollin' out the charm."

"Can't blame him for that. You're a beautiful woman."

She chuckled. "Thank you, but I don't think this is about my looks."

"No, he also likes you."

"That's good to hear." She reached for Spilled Milk's bridle. "I'll take charge of this guy, now."

"Okay." Zach turned the gelding over to her and they started back to the barn. "Sarah picked a great horse for you."

"She did. She seemed eager for me to have a good time out there." They walked in silence for a moment. "Isn't Jack the one who suggested to you that I could open a practice in Shoshone?"

"Actually, it was Regan, but it turns out Jack would be very happy if you did that."

"Do the Chances have a good lawyer? I never thought to ask."

"They do, but he's retiring."

"Aha! No wonder Jack and Sarah are bein' so nice to me."

He tethered Bertha Mae to the hitching post and began unsaddling her. "It's not only because you're a lawyer."

"I know. They wouldn't want me around if they didn't like me, so that's gratifyin'. But my profession doesn't hurt my cause."

"Guess not." From the corner of his eye he observed her efficiency as she unsaddled the gelding and set both blanket and saddle on the hitching post as he'd done. She'd be right at home on a working ranch.

She paused to glance over at him. "Did Jack ask you to get back into law? He must have. It'd solve their problem."

"He did."

"And what did you say?" Hope glimmered in her eyes.

He met her gaze. "I told him no."

16

Jeannette hadn't expected Zach to have a sudden change of heart, but she wished he'd at least say he was willing to give the idea some thought. "I'm sure he was disappointed to hear that."

"I'm sure he was." He shrugged. "But I don't want to hold out false hope to the guy."

Or to her, either. He hadn't said that, but she was a smart woman. She could figure it out.

He broke eye contact. "I'll bring out the brushes so you can start on that while I put away the tack."

"Okay." She watched him heft Bertha Mae's saddle and walk into the barn. Too bad he looked so damned good doing it. She'd have an easier time being upset with him if he didn't look so gorgeous.

His jeans and sweat-stained T-shirt fit as if he'd been sewn into them. With his scuffed boots and his dusty hat, he looked a lot more like a cowboy than a lawyer. If she didn't know better, she'd swear he'd been doing this job all his adult life.

For the first time she wondered if she'd misjudged the situation. Maybe Zach would finish out his days as a ranch hand and be perfectly content. It was his life, after all, and if that was what he wanted, that was what he should get.

He reappeared with a plastic carryall that she found quite familiar. It could have come out of her parents' barn. As a kid she'd loved using the brushes, curry combs and hoof picks, but then she'd had her debut.

After that rite of passage had been completed, her mother had insisted a young lady shouldn't be mucking out stalls and grooming horses. The Trentons had employees to handle those chores. Jeannette had been taught never to lose sight of the fact she was a Trenton.

At the time she hadn't put up a fight. But as she brushed the gelding's brown-and-white coat and pulled a comb through his mane, she realized that her mother had deprived her of something she'd loved, all in the name of gentility. Fortunately the attitude was different on the Last Chance. Women were encouraged, even expected, to help take care of the horses.

After Zach had stowed the tack, he returned and picked up a brush. "When I saw you in the barn that first day, I recognized your love of horses, but I didn't know you had experience taking care of them."

"I learned everything I know before I became a Southern belle and was told working down at the stables wasn't ladylike."

"What were you supposed to do, sit on the porch and drink mint juleps?"

"Pretty much. Come to think of it, how did you get so comfortable with horses?"

"When I was in college, I worked as a camp counselor during the summer. Somehow I was put in charge of the horses we had at the camp, and I loved it. But once I became involved in building a law practice, I forgot about horses." Dust flew as he stroked the brush across the mare's flanks.

She watched the way he worked. He did have an affinity for the job.

"Anyway, when I finally started questioning my life, I remembered how much fun I'd had caring for these guys every summer. I set out to find a ranch that would hire me."

"And ended up at the Last Chance, obviously."

"Luckily, yes. I'd heard wonderful things about the place. Thank God Jack was willing to give an inexperienced cowhand a trial run."

She tore her gaze away from the sight of his muscles flexing beneath the thin T-shirt. "It's easy to see why you love it here."

"Then you must also see why I don't want to give it up for a desk job."

She started to say something and thought better of it. Obviously he believed that opening a law practice in Shoshone would ruin his cherished life as a cowhand. Maybe it would. He might be an all-or-nothing kind of guy who could either be a gung-ho lawyer or a laid-back cowboy, but not both.

Even so, she couldn't shake the notion that this life wasn't a perfect fit for him. When Jack had magnanimously given him the rest of the day off, he'd winced as if he didn't like being reminded of his employee status. The reaction had been subtle, something no one else might have caught. But she was invested in him now and was attuned to his moods.

She couldn't resist prodding him to see if she could get that reaction again. "It was considerate of Jack to give you the rest of the day off and switch your free day, too."

"Yep, it was." Zach tossed the brush in the carrier. "I appreciate it." His response was totally appropriate, but there was a slight edge to his voice as if he had to force himself to say that.

Maybe that meant nothing and he'd get over his resentment of being subject to the impulses of his boss. Jack seemed like an excellent boss and his whims were probably benign. Yet he held the power.

Zach was by nature a leader and an independent thinker who'd spent years being in control of his working hours. If losing that control continued to bother him, even at a subconscious level, his resentment could fester. He might not notice the change as bitterness crept into his soul, but if she hung around, she would.

"About done?"

Startled out of her thoughts, she discovered that she was standing motionless, the brush resting against her horse's flank while she stared into space. "Almost." She began brushing vigorously, so vigorously that Spilled Milk turned his head to gaze at her as if wondering if someone had given her a jump start. "I was daydreaming."

"I hope it was about taking a solar shower when we get back. I'm looking forward to that."

That thought galvanized her even more, but she wasn't sure that shower was in their future. "Didn't we use up the water yesterday?"

"I refilled it before I left this morning. That's my routine. Then it can warm up during the heat of the day and be ready when I get home."

She peered over her horse's rump and discovered Zach watching her with a telltale glow in his eyes. For sure he was thinking about having sex in that shower, and now she was, too. Her body tightened in anticipation as she quickly finished grooming Spilled Milk. "Done."

"Great. I'll take the brush." He came over to get it, walked back and leaned down to drop it in the plastic carrier. His lithe movements seemed particularly sexy today.

But then anything he did might seem sexy right now. She was imagining him naked under the shower in the golden light of late afternoon. That image would probably haunt her in the days ahead, and if she had any sense, she'd let him take that shower alone.

Apparently she had no sense, because she'd already decided to join him there and revel in the experience one more time. After they turned both horses out into the pasture, they climbed into their respective vehicles. He'd suggested that she lead now that she knew where she was going. That way he'd get her dust instead of vice versa.

She accepted his gallantry, although she suspected he had an agenda just like Jack and Sarah. He wanted her to move here to be with him. In the next fifteen hours or so, he'd pull out all the stops and she would be tempted to give in. She already knew that, too.

Giving in would be a mistake, but she needed to be clear in her mind about that before his loving wiped out all her noble intentions. She had the space of this drive to shore up her defenses.

The timing was wrong—not so much for her, but for him. She was ready to make a major change in her life and a small practice in a little town like Shoshone sounded exactly right. Zach was convinced he knew his future path and maybe he did, but she wasn't buying it.

He needed to figure things out on his own, though. In the end, everyone did. She'd get out of his way and let him do that. She didn't know how long it would take, or if he'd ever change his mind about practicing law. Maybe she and Zach had no future.

That thought was horribly painful, but she should face the possibility with a plan. Thank God she did have savings, because that would help. Once she was back in Virginia she'd begin the process of leaving her old life behind.

She'd notify the firm and stay on long enough for an orderly transfer of her caseload. She'd begin packing up everything she planned to take with her. In her spare time, she'd study for the Wyoming bar exam.

Because she needed an alternative if Shoshone didn't work out, she'd research other small towns in Wyoming that might be good places to settle. All of that would take several weeks, weeks in which Zach might have an epiphany. If not, she'd journey on her own to whatever spot seemed the most like Shoshone to begin her new life.

Her convictions firmly in place, she parked near the Airstream and climbed out. Zach pulled his truck in behind her car. She'd barely had time to draw a breath before he was out of the truck.

Setting his hat on the truck's dusty fender, he strode toward her, his gaze purposeful. "Shower time."

She laughed as he pulled her into his arms. "We need to go inside first."

"No, we don't." He took off her straw hat and put it on the hood of her car. "We can strip down right here. I do it all the time." He grinned as he slipped his hands up the back of her shirt and deftly unhooked her bra. "But doing it with you will be way more fun."

Her heartbeat sped up. "What about towels?"

"It's warm. We'll air dry." He pulled her shirt over her head and tossed it next to her hat.

Undressing outside shouldn't be any different from yesterday when she'd walked out of the Airstream naked. Yet somehow it felt more daring, maybe because of the intensity in his gray eyes as he slid her bra straps down her arms.

"I love looking at you."

Her nipples tightened beneath his hungry gaze. "I love lookin' at you, too." She reached for the hem of his T-shirt, tugged the shirt over his head and threw it in the general direction of her car. She had no idea where it landed because she was too busy drinking in the sight of his bronzed chest.

"Come here." He drew her forward, watching as her nipples made contact and quivered against his warm skin. "Your breathing just changed."

"So did yours." Their rapid breaths created a sensuous friction that made her tremble with excitement, yet they were barely touching.

With a groan he pulled her against the solid wall of his chest. "Damn. I want you so much."

"I want you, too." She flattened her hands over the firm muscles of his back and gazed up at him. "We could go inside and save the shower for later."

His fingers flexed against the denim covering her

backside. "We can save the shower for later, but we don't have to go inside."

The implication made her slick with desire, but she wanted more than a climax. She wanted to feel him deep within her, thrusting rhythmically until that shared moment of release. "We need to go inside for what I want."

"Maybe not." He backed her against the car and unbuckled her belt. "Tell me what you want."

"This." She cupped him through his jeans. His erection strained against the zipper. "All of this."

He gulped in air. "Okay, then." He abandoned his quest to unfasten her jeans, reached into his pocket and pulled out a condom. "Please watch over that."

"Zach! You just happened to have a—"

"No mystery there." He knelt down and expertly pulled off her boots one at a time. "Shoved it in my pocket before I left this morning. Wanted to be ready for anything." He stood and cupped her face in both hands. "Looks like it was a good decision." His mouth claimed hers in a short but very passionate kiss that left no doubt where this episode was headed.

He didn't waste any time getting there, either. Her jeans and panties joined the rest of the clothes on the hood of her car. Then he unfastened his jeans to reveal how ready he was.

Desire shot through her, hot and demanding. She reached for him, needing to touch that stiff, sleek answer to her lustful prayers. A drop of moisture had gathered at the tip. She wanted—

"No." He caught her wrist. "I might come."

She moaned softly in frustration as his beauty was covered with latex.

His breathing grew more labored. "Then I...I couldn't give you what you want." He swallowed. "Grab hold of my shoulders."

As she did, he bracketed her hips and lifted her up against the fender. Her breath caught as he pressed her against the warm metal. The sensation of that metal on her bare skin was so erotic that her body clenched in response.

"Wrap your legs around me." Urgency sharpened his tone.

She didn't have to be asked twice. She desperately needed the gift he was about to bestow.

He held her steady, took a shaky breath and slid in. The motion required no time and almost no effort. "You're drenched."

She exhaled slowly and fought to keep from coming right that very second. She looked into his eyes, dark as thunderclouds. "It's...no mystery," she said, repeating his words.

"Guess not." He held her gaze. "Just be still for a bit."

She nodded.

He gave her a crooked smile. "Never tried this before." He took another ragged breath. "Don't want to...rush it."

"Me, either."

His glance traveled over her. It lingered on her hair, her lips and her breasts. "You look so good in the sunlight. Like you're glowing."

"Maybe I am."

"I'd believe it." His voice was husky. "Especially there." His gaze continued downward and settled at the juncture of her thighs. "Where the fire is." His cock twitched.

Unable to help herself, she tightened in response.

"Ahhh." He sucked in a breath and tensed. Then he relaxed slightly and looked into her eyes. "What you do to me, Jeannette."

"The same thing you do to me, Zach."

"And do you know how great that is?"

"Yes."

"I've never made love to a woman outside up against a car. Only you could inspire me to do that."

"Only you could talk me into it."

"I know." Holding her gaze, he eased out and pushed back again. "We're good together." He initiated a slow rhythm.

"Uh-huh." She was in no position to argue. But she was in a perfect position to receive the kind of pleasure that he excelled at giving. Each thrust took her higher until she began to whimper.

He pumped faster. "We…belong together."

"Mmm." She'd lost the ability to form words. Nothing mattered but the steady beat of his powerful strokes. They drove her to the edge of sanity and touched off little explosions every time he sank into her quivering channel.

"You're almost there." He was panting, now. "I can feel it. I know you, Jeannette. *I know you.*"

"Yes."

"Come for me."

"Yes…yes…*yes*." Sweet surrender. A release so strong her body was wracked with the pulsing rush of it as she gasped and breathlessly chanted his name.

"I'm here. I'm here, love." With a deep groan, he rocked forward and shuddered against her.

I'm here, love. His words echoed in her mind as she held him and absorbed the aftershocks of his climax. She couldn't argue with those words, either. She was his love. And he was hers. No matter how it all turned out, that much would still be true.

17

FOR THE PAST MONTH, Zach had looked forward to each morning. Until this one. He and Jeannette hadn't slept much, but they'd had plenty of sex, more than he'd thought possible for one night.

In between the incredible bouts of sex, they'd rested and talked. He had no doubt she was as much in love with him as he was with her. But that didn't seem to matter any more than the great sex. She wouldn't agree to move to Shoshone.

Instead she insisted that he needed more time to adjust to his new way of life. What she really meant was that he needed time to grow bored. She'd never come right out and said that, but he'd picked up on it, anyway.

As daylight approached, he considered whether professing his love openly would change her mind. He decided that it wouldn't, so why put himself in such a vulnerable position? Instead he made love to her once more for what could be the last time.

He tried not to dwell on that as he got up, pulled on his jeans and made coffee. She showered in the tiny bathroom, and he stayed away from that end of the trailer when she left the bathroom to dress in the hallway. Watching her do that would make him want to touch her and coax her back to bed, which wouldn't accomplish anything—except maybe make her miss her flight.

At one point he'd thought about doing that on purpose. She'd probably be upset with him, though, and he'd only delay the inevitable. He couldn't expect Jack to give him a second day off, either.

Somehow he had to get through the next hour or so before she left. He felt the urge to do something for her, so he scrambled eggs and made toast to go with the coffee. "Breakfast is ready!" he called out.

"Oh." She appeared in slacks and a silky-looking blouse, her Virginia lawyer's clothes. She was still in her bare feet and didn't have makeup on yet. "You didn't have to do that."

"And you don't have to eat it. I needed something to occupy my time." He sounded surly, which wasn't how he wanted her to remember him. He managed a smile. "Never mind. I'll put it out for the raccoons."

"No, you won't." She padded into the kitchen. "I'd love some breakfast."

"Then have a seat and I'll bring it to you. I hope you like your eggs scrambled."

"I do."

Spatula in one hand and a plate in the other, he glanced at her. "Would you tell me if you didn't?"

"Yes. Scrambled is how I make them at home."

"Which you hardly ever do, I'll bet." He knew she wasn't a cook.

"Hardly ever, and even then in the microwave."

"Jeannette, if you're eating this breakfast to be nice, then please don't." Okay, he still sounded surly but he couldn't seem to help it.

"I'm eating this breakfast because you fixed it for me, which has nothing to do with being nice. I'm doing it because I—" She ended the sentence abruptly and her cheeks turned pink.

He understood what people meant when they talked about heartache. His chest hurt something fierce. "Because you what?" he asked softly.

Pressing her lips together, she shook her head.

"It won't kill you to say it, you know."

She swallowed. "I don't want to make things worse."

"I don't think they can get much worse."

"Zach…"

"Oh, what the hell. I love you, Jeannette. You know it and I know it. And what's more, you love me, which was what you almost said just now." He heard the anger and frustration in his voice and sighed. "That's not how those words are supposed to be said, either. Sorry about that."

"I…I have to go." She got up from the table and hurried out of the kitchen.

As he listened to her throwing things in her suitcase and banging around in her haste to leave, he stared at the spatula and plate he was holding. How he'd love to hurl the plate at the nearest wall and howl like the wolves that roamed the nearby hills. But he didn't want to leave her with that image of him, either.

So he made sure the burner was turned off and unplugged the coffeepot. He hadn't put on his boots, but it didn't matter. Opening the front door, he walked out on the little stoop and down the steps. Dry pine needles pricked the bottoms of his feet, but he didn't care.

Hands in his pockets, he stared at the Grand Tetons. The timelessness and immensity of those jagged peaks with their whipped-cream topping of snow usually calmed him and gave him perspective. It wasn't working this morning. The peace that he'd found here was gone.

Behind him the trailer door opened. He turned as she came out, purse over her shoulder and pulling her suitcase while she balanced on four-inch heels.

"Let me help." He hurried up the steps and took charge of the suitcase.

"Thank you." She didn't look at him.

He carried the suitcase to her car and heard the click as she used the remote to unlock it. He stowed her case in the backseat and glanced up just as she started to slide behind the wheel. "Whoa, whoa." He rounded the car and grasped her arm. "Come back out of there for a minute. You can't just get in and drive away."

She glanced up at him. "I think it's for the best."

"I promise not to say anything that will make you uncomfortable, but we deserve a proper goodbye."

She was silent for a moment, and then she got out of the car and faced him. "Goodbye, Zach."

"You're acting like you're in front of a firing squad."

"It feels a little like that."

"Well, it's not like that." Stepping forward, he cupped her face in one hand and brushed a strand of hair back from her cheek as he gazed into her emerald-green eyes. "You're an incredible woman, and I'm glad we met."

She took a shaky breath. "So am I."

"Goodbye, Jeannette." Leaning down, he kissed her softly. Then he released her and stepped back.

Her eyes remained closed. With his hands fisted at his sides, he resisted the urge to haul her back into his arms. He wanted to kiss her until she changed her mind and decided to stay, no matter how long that took. The way she looked as she stood there trembling, it wouldn't take long at all.

He let the moment pass. She'd made her wishes clear and he'd only be taking advantage of this difficult moment right before she left. That wouldn't be very noble of him.

She opened her eyes and cleared her throat. "Goodbye, Zach." Then she climbed into the car and started the engine.

He should have thought to move the truck to make it easier for her. But she pulled forward and engineered a creative backing job to successfully avoid banging into it. He was impressed, because if she were as wrecked by this parting as he was, she couldn't be all that steady.

Although going into the Airstream would have been far cooler on his part, he stayed where he was until she made it to the dirt road. She beeped the horn once and he raised a hand in farewell. Then she was gone, her tires kicking up dust as she drove away.

He dreaded going back inside, but the sooner he got that over with, the better. Bracing himself for the emptiness he'd find there, he climbed the steps and walked through the door. He'd expected silence. He'd expected the memories to flood him.

He hadn't expected her scent to greet him the minute he walked in. It was a subtle perfume, a cross between a spice and a floral. He hadn't consciously taken note of it while they'd been together, but it hit him like a sledgehammer now.

Torn between throwing open all the windows to let it out and closing them tight to keep it in, he did neither. Instead he quickly put on socks and boots, pulled on a T-shirt and poured himself a cup of coffee. Then he started toward the door. He'd sit outside and read for a while.

But he turned back when he realized the plan required reading material. Crossing to his bookshelf, he looked through the offerings. He grabbed a camping magazine he hadn't finished. Then, for reasons he didn't want to examine too closely, he also took the study guide for the bar exam.

Unfolding one of his camp chairs, he picked a spot in the shade of a pine tree and settled in. With luck, he'd become absorbed in his reading and get past the crushing impact of Jeannette's departure. First he picked up the magazine.

Jumping from one article to the next, he searched for something that would engage him and help him forget his troubles for a little while. Nothing in the magazine accomplished that. With a sigh, he tossed it down and reached for the study guide. That probably wouldn't work, either.

Hours later, his stomach rumbled, reminding him that he hadn't eaten anything. To his complete astonishment, he'd made it almost halfway through the study guide. He was fascinated by the similarities and the differences between California's bar exam and this one.

More than fascination gripped him, though. He was intellectually excited for the first time in months. He felt a little bit like Rip Van Winkle waking up from a long sleep.

He wanted to finish the study guide and then read through it again to make sure he had a handle on it. But mostly he wanted to take that bar exam, if for no other reason than to see if he could pass it as easily as he expected he could. He didn't have to tell anyone about it, though.

Assuming he got his license to practice law in Wyoming, he could decide at that point whether to do anything with it. Maybe passing the exam would be enough for him. It would be his secret project, and he'd take one step at a time. Ironically, this kind of challenge might be the only one capable of taking his mind off Jeannette.

A PACKING BOX sat on the floor of Jeannette's kitchen along with a pile of brown wrapping paper. She stood in front of her cupboard of dishes. They were lovely and expensive, a complete set of twelve she'd bought soon after being hired at the law firm.

The pattern of tiny flowers and vines curled gracefully around the edge of each plate, saucer and cup. Several years ago she'd thought these dishes were the height of gracious living. Unfortunately, they didn't fit the person she was now. In her new life she imagined a table filled with chunky pottery in bold colors.

She thought of Erin, her former assistant at the

law firm. Erin would love these dishes. That decision made, Jeannette started wrapping the dishes and tucking them in the box, although they wouldn't go with her out west. They'd stay where they belonged in Virginia. She'd buy a new set of dishes when she arrived in…wherever she decided to go.

Four weeks had passed since she'd left Wyoming, and she'd heard nothing from Zach. She'd researched other towns as planned, but she'd held off choosing one of those alternatives. Her lease had another month to run, so she was in no big rush to make that decision.

Her hope that Zach would come through might be fading, but it hadn't totally disappeared. He could still call. What a shame if she rented a U-Haul and moved prematurely. So she'd taken her time with packing, which had allowed her to be more thoughtful about what she was taking, and what she was leaving behind. Like these dishes, for example.

The cupboard was nearly empty when her cell phone rang. She picked it up from the charger on the small desk in the kitchen without thinking much about the call. She'd been handling lots of details recently that had required many phone calls. Then she saw the name on the screen and felt light-headed.

She was breathless as she answered and didn't care. "Zach?"

"You *quit* the law firm?"

"Uh, yeah. And by the way, I'm fine. How are you?"

"Ticked off! When were you planning to tell me you quit?"

"Whenever you called." She took a calming breath.

"So here you are, and now you know. How are things in Shoshone?"

"They were fine when I left."

"You left? So where are you now?"

"Outside your door."

The phone still to her ear, she raced to her front door, flipped the latch on the lock and swung it open. Sure enough, there he stood wearing his best cowboy clothes and that black Stetson he called his party hat.

He held up the study guide for the Wyoming bar, a duplicate of the one she had on her bookshelf. "And while we're discussing stealth moves, what were you thinking writing a message on the next-to-last page?"

"I didn't want you to see it until you were almost done." Her chest grew tight. He was here, but what did that mean, exactly? "Did you…did you read it?"

"We can discuss that later. Right now I need a place to stay. I figured since I put you up, you might be willing to return the favor."

"Of course."

"Great." He picked up a small duffel she hadn't noticed because she was so busy feasting on the sight of him and making bargains with herself. He'd at least read to the end of the study guide. That might be enough for now. If he'd done that, then he couldn't be totally opposed to taking the exam, and with some encouragement, that could lead to—

"Can I come in through this door, or are you planning to send me around to some other entrance?"

"Oh!" She stepped back so he could walk in. "Sorry. I'm still gettin' used to the fact that you're actually here." She breathed in the scent of him. Oh, yeah. Reading the study guide was plenty. She would work with that.

"Good thing I showed up before you moved and left no forwarding address." He dropped his duffel on the floor along with the study guide.

She closed the door and turned to discover he'd taken off his hat and laid that on top of the duffel. "I wouldn't have moved without—"

"God, Jeannette!" He pulled her into his arms and kissed her with a desperation that made her heart sing. When he lifted his lips from hers, he continued to pepper her face with kisses. "I thought you'd already made partner, and because it's a weekday, I went to your office, but they said you'd quit, and I had to sign my life away to get your address, but Erin came through for me because she remembered who I was."

"Erin's a sweetheart."

"Yes, she is, but *you*." He pulled back to glare at her. "You are one devious woman. What in hell's going on with you?"

"I'm leaving Virginia."

"And your destination would be?"

"Now that you're here, I'm thinking Shoshone."

He stared at her. "But you said you wouldn't move there until I got my act together."

She wound her arms around his neck. "I know, but if you read through the study guide, you're at least considerin' the possibility of a law career. That's close enough."

"It is? Damn. I could have saved myself a lot of work."

"What does that mean?"

"I just got the word. I passed the bar in Wyoming."

"You did?" She hugged him tight. "That's fantastic!"

"There's more."

"More?" She leaned back to gaze into his face. "Like what?"

"I rented some office space in town."

"Zach! You're really doin' it."

"Guess so." He cupped her bottom as if he had the right to.

She decided he did. "What about your job at the ranch?"

"I'll put in some time on weekends, but Jack would much rather have me as his lawyer than his ranch hand. I'm also thinking I might buy some horse property in the area so I can own a couple of saddle horses. I came here thinking you'd be settled into your partnership and wouldn't be interested in joining my new firm, but I had to at least ask, and now I—"

"I'm so in."

He grinned at her. "You do realize you have to pass the bar exam."

"Been studyin'."

"Oh, really?"

"Ever since I left. I've just been waitin' for you, cowboy."

"You have put me through it, lady."

"For your own good. You never would have come to this decision if I hadn't given you some space to figure it out."

He sighed. "You could be right about that. But writing what you did near the back of the study guide? That was…"

"All I could think to do." She'd been frantic to

leave, but at the last minute she'd pulled his study guide from the bookshelf and scribbled *I love you* near the end of the book. "And I meant it."

He tugged her in closer. "You do realize how that incriminates you, right? I now have written proof."

"Are you going to use it against me?"

"You bet. Now you have to marry me."

"I thought you might insist on that."

"Any objections, counselor?"

"Not a one. It's time to make this legal." She smiled up at him. "I love you, Zachary Powell."

"I know you do." He feathered a kiss over her lips. "I have it in writing."

Epilogue

BEN RADCLIFFE HAD been itching for a challenge, and Jack Chance had just brought him one—building a custom saddle that would be a surprise for the woman who received it. That meant Ben wouldn't meet her or the horse who'd wear the saddle until after the job was finished. He'd never attempted such a thing before.

Jack had brought the necessary measurements for the horse and the woman, and he seemed to know roughly what he wanted. The saddle would be a show-stopper embellished with silver and turquoise accents. Jack was prepared to pay the price, too. Apparently his extended family was chipping in so they could afford to be extravagant.

"I realize this is somewhat short notice." Jack wandered around the shop and paused to inspect each of the three saddles Ben was currently working on. "My brothers and I had a hell of a time figuring out what would make a good seventieth birthday present for her. She's…special."

"I'm sure she is." Years ago Ben would have felt a

pang of envy at hearing some guy praise his mother with such obvious affection. Now he felt nothing at all.

"Anyway, once we decided on a saddle designed specifically for her favorite horse, Bertha Mae, I asked around. Everyone said there was this guy in Sheridan who hadn't been in business that long but he did fine work." Jack glanced at Ben. "I like what I see, and I also like the idea of patronizing someone who's just starting to get recognized."

"I won't kid you. Making a custom saddle for Sarah Chance and her favorite horse will give me bragging rights."

Jack met his gaze. "If you do a good job, I'll spread the word myself."

"I'd appreciate that."

"But we're already well into October. And we want this to be a fancy-ass saddle. Can you do it?"

Ben looked at the Remington calendar tacked on the wall. "You said her birthday's December nineteenth, right?"

"Yeah."

"I can do it."

"Excellent. Also, I need you to deliver it to the ranch, but not too soon, because we'll have to hide it. I hate to say this, but her grandchildren can't keep a secret worth a damn."

"Understood. I should show up around the eighteenth, then."

"That would be perfect, assuming the weather cooperates."

"I have a four-by-four truck and I'm used to driving in snow."

"Normal snow, sure, but a blizzard could muck things up. I suppose, worst-case scenario, you could email a picture and we could show her on a tablet at her birthday dinner, but that's not what I'm going for."

"I'll make it over there."

Jack gave him a long look. "I believe you will. And I hope you can stay for the party so you can see her face when she gets her first glimpse of it."

"I'd like that."

"It's Christmas week, though. If you have to get back, I understand."

"Not really." Then he wished he hadn't said that. In his life Christmas was just another day, but when he admitted that, people tended to feel sorry for him. "I mean, I can shift things around if necessary. It's the beauty of being single."

Jack smiled. "I remember those days." He stepped forward and held out his hand. "Then we have a deal."

"Yes, we do." Ben grasped his hand. "You'll see me on the eighteenth. Will I need a cover story?"

"Oh, yeah." Jack rubbed his chin. "Just pretend you're there to buy a horse. Mom will be so busy with Christmas preparations she won't pay much attention. But I'll have a room made up so you can stay a couple of nights."

"Looking forward to it." Because his own family was a complete disaster, he was fascinated with the idea that some might actually work.

The Chance clan's devotion to their matriarch indicated they might be such a family. Making the saddle for her would be good for business. Helping celebrate her birthday at the Last Chance Ranch would be a nice bonus.

* * * * *

COMING NEXT MONTH FROM

 HARLEQUIN®

 *Blaze*®

Available August 19, 2014

#811 A SEAL'S FANTASY
Unrated!
by Tawny Weber
Navy SEAL Dominic Castillo has a reputation for always getting the girl—but he meets his match when forced to protect Lara Banks, the tempting, unrepentant sister of his rival.

#812 BEHIND CLOSED DOORS
Made in Montana
by Debbi Rawlins
Sexy rancher Nathan Landers steers clear of Blackfoot Falls and the small-town rumor mill, but beautiful newcomer Bethany Wilson is offering a naughty no-strings deal he can't refuse!

#813 CABIN FEVER
The Wrong Bed
by Jillian Burns
On a cruise, fashion blogger Carly Pendleton tries to fight her attraction to "Average Joe" contest winner Joe Tedesco, who sizzles with raw masculinity. They don't seem to have much in common...but can she fight the fire blazing between them?

#814 STRIPPED DOWN
Pleasure Before Business
by Kelli Ireland
One impulsive night with gorgeous dancer Dalton Chase leaves engineer Cassidy Jameson aching for more. But inviting him into her bed is one thing...inviting him into her life, quite another.

YOU CAN FIND MORE INFORMATION ON UPCOMING HARLEQUIN® TITLES, FREE EXCERPTS AND MORE AT WWW.HARLEQUIN.COM.

HBCNM0814

REQUEST YOUR FREE BOOKS!
2 FREE NOVELS PLUS 2 FREE GIFTS!

Entering her building, Lara felt the weight of the day on her shoulders. She still had hours of homework and eight shows to dance over the weekend. If she nailed this assignment, she'd have the top grade in the class, which meant an internship with a top-flight security firm.

Six more weeks to go. With a sigh, she rounded the hallway to her corridor.

Lara Lee, Cyber Detective.

She grinned, then blinked. Frowning, she noted the hall lighting was out. She'd just put her key in the lock when she felt him.

It wasn't his body heat that tipped her off.

Nope, it was the lust swirling through her system, making her knees weak and her nipples ache.

Taking a deep breath, she turned. "Do you always lurk in the shadows?"

"Hall light is out. Shadows are all you've got here."

"What do you want?"

"I told you. I need to talk to you about your brother."

HBEXP79815

"And I told you. I don't have a brother."

Not anymore.

"Lieutenant Phillip Banks. Navy SEAL. Ring any bells?" His words were easy, the look in his eyes as mellow as the half smile on his full lips.

"My last name is Lee." Then, before she could stop herself, she asked, "Why are you running errands for this guy, anyway?"

His dark eyes flashed. "Sweetheart, do I look like anyone's errand boy?" he said.

Lara couldn't resist.

She let her eyes wander down the long, hard length of his body. Broad shoulders and a drool-worthy chest tapered into flat abs, narrow hips and strong thighs.

She wet her lips and met his eyes again.

He looked hot.

As if he'd like to strip her down and play show-and-tell.

Tempting, since she'd bet that'd would be worth seeing.

"Sorry," she said. "I'm not the woman you're looking for."

Damn.

Not for the first time in his life, Dominic Castillo cursed Banks. The guy was a pain. Figured that long, lean and sexy was just as bad.

He wanted to grab her, haul her off to the nearest horizontal surface.

Insane.

He was on a mission. *She* was his duty.

He'd never lusted after a mission before.

Pick up A SEAL'S FANTASY by Tawny Weber, available in September 2014 wherever you buy Harlequin® Blaze® books.

HBEXP79815

Can They Take the Heat?

On a cruise, fashion blogger Carly Pendleton tries to fight her attraction to "Average Joe" contest winner Joe Tedesco, who sizzles with raw masculinity. They don't seem to have much in common...but can she fight the fire blazing between them?

From the reader-favorite *The Wrong Bed* miniseries

Cabin Fever
by *Jillian Burns*

Available September 2014 wherever you buy Harlequin Blaze books.

HARLEQUIN®

A *Romance* FOR EVERY MOOD™

Stay up-to-date on all your
romance-reading news with the
Harlequin Shopping Guide,
featuring bestselling authors, exciting new
miniseries, books to watch and more!

The newest issue will be delivered right to you
with our compliments! There are 4 each year.

Signing up is easy.

EMAIL

ShoppingGuide@Harlequin.ca

WRITE TO US

HARLEQUIN BOOKS
Attention: Customer Service Department
P.O. Box 9057, Buffalo, NY 14269-9057

OR PHONE

1-800-873-8635 in the United States
1-888-343-9777 in Canada

Please allow 4-6 weeks for delivery of the first issue by mail.